Olivia's Eyes Half-Closed In A Sultry Expression That Took Matt's Breath Away.

"Let's get this out of the way between us, right now...." he said softly, leaning closer.

She slanted him a sensual look that set his pulse pounding. He slipped his arm around her waist and heard her gasp. She was soft, warm, all curves. He took his time, giving her a chance to pull away or protest.

Somewhere in the depths of his being, he knew he was crossing a line, going against everything he'd sworn to do. But he couldn't resist, even if he knew in his heart that he was opening himself up for unending trouble.

Even if he was damned for it, he was going to kiss her....

Dear Reader,

What happens when a determined, "take-charge" male clashes with an independent, "mistress-of-my-own-destiny" woman?

I wanted to explore two strong-willed people who had opposing goals and dreams. What happens when they charge head-on into each other's lives? Each one has plans for the future that are changed totally by the other person. Sparks fly, burned away in the fiery attraction that develops between them and ignites passion.

Pregnant with the First Heir introduces the Ransome family, Matt Ransome, the oldest son, and Olivia Brennan, a woman with no family. I couldn't resist writing about that hard, cynical male who hides his soft heart until a woman comes along who can dissolve the barriers and win his trust and love.

Family dynamics are always interesting to me. The majority of my books involve families in the background of the story, and *Pregnant with the First Heir* launches THE WEALTHY RANSOMES series about two Ransome brothers and their younger sister.

So, dear reader, please turn the page and enter the world of Matt Ransome and Olivia Brennan, who are getting ready to meet for the first time and toss each other's world into upheaval.

Best wishes,

Sara Orwig

SARA ORWIG

PREGNANT WITH THE FIRST HEIR

Published by Silhouette Books
America's Publisher of Contemporary Romance

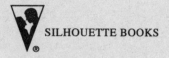 **SILHOUETTE BOOKS**

ISBN-13: 978-0-373-76752-6
ISBN-10:   0-373-76752-8

PREGNANT WITH THE FIRST HEIR

Visit Silhouette Books at www.eHarlequin.com

Printed in U.S.A.

Recent books by Sara Orwig

Silhouette Desire

Cowboy's Special Woman #1449
**Do You Take This Enemy?* #1476
**The Rancher, the Baby &
    the Nanny* #1486
Entangled with a Texan #1547
†*Shut Up and Kiss Me* #1581
†*Standing Outside the Fire* #1594
Estate Affair #1657
‡*Pregnant with the First Heir* #1752

Silhouette Intimate Moments

*One Tough Cowboy #1192
†*Bring on the Night* #1298
†*Don't Close Your Eyes* #1316

*Stallion Pass
†Stallion Pass: Texas Knights
‡The Wealthy Ransomes

SARA ORWIG

lives in Oklahoma. She has a patient husband who will take her on research trips anywhere from big cities to old forts. She is an avid collector of Western history books. With a master's degree in English, Sara has written historical romance, mainstream fiction and contemporary romance. Books are beloved treasures that take Sara to magical worlds, and she loves both reading and writing them.

With many thanks to Melissa Jeglinski and
to Jessica Alvarez.

One

She was born to please a man.

The auburn-haired waitress behind the wooden counter had lush, come-hither looks. Her pouty lips promised sexual gratification. The sensual way of moving her ripe body made a man think of hot sex. Judging by her flat stomach, it was difficult to believe that she was three months pregnant. Her cutoffs revealed long, shapely legs that added to her appeal. At ten o'clock on a July Saturday night, male customers in the smoke-filled Texas honky-tonk constantly watched her move around the room. Matthew Ransome was certain that Olivia Brennan was so accustomed to men staring at her that she wouldn't wonder about his glances.

In the red T-shirt and cutoffs that was her uniform at Two-Steppin' Ribs, she waited on a customer in a nearby booth. Three musicians played country-western music while boot-scooting couples circled the dance floor. Even though he occasionally chatted with passing friends, Matt's attention remained focused on Olivia.

In the time since he had arrived and ordered his rib dinner, slowly eating and sipping one cold beer, Matt had watched half a dozen men hit on her. Some touched her, taking her hand or her wrist, patting her rear. She twisted free, or shaking her head, sidestepped groping hands, and he guessed she was being asked either to go out after work or—judging from the rough crowd—to have sex. He was surprised by her solemnity. She rarely gave more than the most perfunctory smile, not at all what he had imagined about her.

Matt watched locals he knew—Pug Mosley, the manager of the honky-tonk, openly flirted with her and several times during the evening let his hand brush her bottom. Once she spun around, telling him something. He grinned, shrugged and said something in return before he walked away in his usual swagger.

Fighting the urge to step in when Pug talked to Olivia, Matt intended to keep his approach to her low-key.

From what he had learned about her from the Fort Worth private detective he had hired a week ago, she wasn't dating anyone and there hadn't been a man in her life since Matt's brother Jeff. Matt found that difficult to believe except he had great faith in his P.I. With her body and mane of unruly auburn hair, she looked sexy and wild, like a woman with many partners.

Jeff could get mixed up with some shady people and seldom had there been a woman in his life that he had brought home. Including Olivia, who was carrying Jeff's child.

Nearing midnight, another local drifted to Olivia, just as obviously flirting with her as other men had. And received the same reception that was so cold Matt could discern her response without hearing a word of her conversation. Since she had been unreceptive to every man in the place, Matt reassessed his opinion of her as easy. He had never seen a female his younger brother couldn't charm, but Matt was beginning to wonder if Jeff was one of few men with whom she had ever had a relationship. Matt's opinion of her climbed a notch.

A small voice inside Matt insisted that he walk away now and never look back. Logically, he knew he should forget Olivia Brennan, but he couldn't any more than he could stop breathing.

Finally, after midnight, she was alone, standing behind the counter with no one around her. Silently warning himself he was seeking a hell of a lot of trouble, he slid out of the booth and circled the dance floor, crossing the room beneath revolving ceiling fans.

When he stopped in front of her, she looked up at him, turning the full force of big green eyes on him. Even in the dim light of the honky-tonk, he was mesmerized, and for a moment, she seemed as ensnared as he.

Attraction, as hot and tangible as a lightning flash, burst between them. The bar and people around them vanished from Matt's consciousness while he focused totally on her. Desire aroused him, a startling need to explore every inch of her ripe body and her sensual mouth. Once again, he knew why his brother had been attracted to her and why every man in the place seemed aware of her. She exuded a blatant sexuality that was all the more powerful up close.

While seconds passed, she stood as still as he did. Then, inhaling deeply, she turned her head, and the eye contact was broken.

As she started to walk away, Matt regained his wits.

"Wait—" he said. When she paused, he held out his hand. "I'm Jeff's brother Matt."

Her eyes narrowed. "I'm sorry about your brother," she stated coolly without taking Matt's hand. Once again, she moved on.

"Wait a minute. I want to talk to you," Matt said, catching up with her. "When do you get off work?" As silence stretched between them, even in the dim light, he saw the flash of fury in the depths of her eyes.

"Look, Jeff and I parted ways a while back," she said. "I don't know why you found me, but there was no longer anything between Jeff and me. You and I have nothing to talk about." Her words poured out swiftly in a throaty voice that was as sexy as everything else about her.

"There was a baby between you," Matt reminded her. "A baby that you and I will both be related to and need to talk about," Matt continued as his insides coiled in a knot. "I'm the uncle, so you give me a few minutes."

She bit her full underlip with even, white teeth and her mouth tempted him to forget the object of why he intended to talk to her.

"I can't guess what you want. Words won't do you any good," she insisted, shaking her head. "I'm through with your family. I don't want to see any of you." Suddenly she leaned closer, lowering her voice. "If you think I'm giving up my baby, you can forget it!" She turned her back and started to walk away.

Momentarily taken aback, Matt stepped in front of her, blocking her way. "I'm the baby's blood relative. You can't dismiss me like that. I want to talk—when and wherever you agree to. If you don't consent, we'll discuss the baby in a court of law. Take your pick."

Glaring at him, she visibly bristled. As she inhaled deeply, he was aware of the strain of the red shirt across her lush breasts. "I don't get off here until two in the morning when we close," she said.

"I'll wait. I promise you, we're going to have a discussion."

"All right. Two o'clock in the parking lot," she said in a level tone of voice even as her eyes sparked with fury.

"Fine. In the meantime, you can bring me some coffee. I'm in a booth on the other side of the room."

Nodding, she walked away and he couldn't keep from watching the sway of her hips.

She turned and slanted him a look over her shoulder, catching him watching her. He clamped his lips together. She had to be aware of the effect she had on men. At least she hadn't been coming after him for money which had surprised him because as soon as he learned about the pregnancy from Jeff, that's what he had expected.

"Damn, Jeff," Matt said under his breath, anger and pain mingling as he thought about his reckless younger brother whose wild lifestyle had caught up with him when he'd died climbing mountains in the Himalayas.

Matt dallied over the cup of coffee until it was obvious that closing time approached. As he stepped to the cash register, Olivia lingered to take his money.

"You can wait out front," she said, giving him another blast of her mesmerizing green eyes. Her low, seductive voice glided hotly over his every nerve. "Employees park in the back and when I'm finished closing, I'll drive my car around to the front. Our chat has to be brief. It's late, and I've had a long day."

He nodded. When he stepped outside, he heard the lock click in the door behind him as it shut. Yellow light from a tall lamp shed a bright glow over the graveled lot. Beneath a sliver of July moon a south breeze tugged at locks of his black hair.

Wondering how long it would take to close, Matt strolled behind the wooden building. Brown paint peeled in spots and the big blue trash bin overflowed with cartons and bottles. Another light on a tall post shone over the graveled area. Three ancient cars with assorted dents and scrapes were parked in the back. Matt's jaw tightened with disgust when he looked at the empty lot. Beyond the circle of light was a field with a grove of scrub oaks. Without security of any sort, the lot was no place for a woman alone at two in the morning.

Matt waited while the employees locked up, dimmed the lights and left, two women and a man coming out at the same time. As the burly man started toward Matt, Olivia caught his arm and said something to him. Giving Matt a long look, the man walked to his car. While the man and woman climbed into separate cars and drove out of the lot, Matt strolled over to Olivia. She stood with her hands on her hips.

"Jeff and I split. I don't think you and I have much to talk about."

"You're carrying his child. He told me and he was certain the baby was his."

"This is his baby, all right," she said. Her face was bathed in light, and Matt could see the fire dancing in her eyes and hear the anger in her tone which heightened his own irritation over her uncooperative attitude.

"Look, I'm related to your baby. Jeff told me you don't have any family and you're on your own. I want to help you."

"Thanks, but no thanks. You don't owe me anything, and I'll take care of my baby," she declared stiffly with a toss of her head that sent her thick mane swirling across her shoulders.

"Why make it more difficult for yourself and for the baby?"

"Jeff didn't want any responsibility for his child. Far from it. His exact words were: 'I don't want to ever know or even see your kid,'" she flung at Matt, and pain stabbed him. "He told me I should have been more careful. He was right there. I don't want any part of anything or anyone connected to Jeff!" she exclaimed firmly and turned to walk to her car.

Matt bit back angry words. It hurt badly to hear that Jeff had denied his child. Jeff hadn't told him that, but then, his kid brother would have known how Matt would react to such news.

Matt hurried ahead of her and blocked her from getting into her car.

"Get out of my way," she said.

"I want to talk. Surely you can give me a few minutes."

She inhaled deeply, and he resisted letting his gaze lower to her full breasts, but it was an effort.

"All right, for only a few more minutes." She crossed her arms over her middle and raised her chin and he knew he was in for a fight.

"This baby will be the only one of the next generation in my family."

"You can't have children?" she asked.

"I'm not a marrying man. I'll never marry anyone."

"That didn't slow your brother down. And he didn't care if this baby was the last of your family. Blood relations didn't seem important to him," she said, and Matt could easily hear the bitterness in her voice. Her fists were clenched, and he realized instead of a rift between Jeff and Olivia, Jeff had created a bottomless chasm. She was all but shaking with fury.

SARA ORWIG   13

Matt fought to bank his own anger that she was being so almighty unreasonable when he offered help that she seemed to desperately need.

"As I recall, there were several of you—a brother, Nick, a sister, Katherine. Can't they produce grandchildren?"

Matt shrugged. "Perhaps someday, but who knows? Nick and Katherine are on the wild side and not likely to settle down soon."

"Like Jeff," Olivia said with bitterness in her voice again.

"None of us is as wild as Jeff was," Matt snapped. "Jeff took whatever he wanted and indulged himself. He thought he was invincible, but it turned out that he wasn't."

"Look, I'm trying to help—"

She shook her head. "No, you're not. You want something. If it's my baby, forget it. And don't think you can go to court and get my precious baby. I'll fight you every inch of the way."

"Will you listen to me?" he said patiently, and she arched her eyebrows.

"I'll listen, but you're on limited time that's growing shorter."

Matt wanted to shake her. Instead, he nodded. "I'm sure you don't make much money as a waitress here. I want to take care of you and the baby financially."

"I don't need your help. End of conversation. You have no claim on me. If you want to go to court over it—go. Since you're not the father, you won't have a strong case. They would give a father rights, but an uncle? I'm willing to take that chance. You stay out of my life. Your brother was a jerk! Now get out of my way."

She slid into her car, slammed and locked the door. The engine rumbled to life with a persistent knock. She backed up, swung in a circle and drove away, crunching gravel beneath the tires.

"Dammit!" Matt swore and clenched his fists. He strode angrily to his pickup, climbed in and headed toward Rincon, Texas where he knew she lived on the fringe of town.

He would try to talk to her one more time before he called his attorney. Little stubborn witch!

Jeff disowned the baby. Matt gritted his teeth as he reflected that most of his life he hadn't understood his kid brother. Without a doubt, the feelings had been mutual. Matt knew his single parent father had done the best he could, but he had been too indulgent with all of them. Jeff, the youngest, he had spoiled rotten.

Matt drove through the neighborhood of small frame houses with dented, ancient cars parked in front yards and lawns high with weeds. When he reached her darkened house, he discovered that Olivia had not come straight home. She might not be coming home tonight at all.

In disgust, he wondered if she had taken up with a man. He shrugged away the unwanted notion, reminding himself that there hadn't been any mention from the P.I. of a boyfriend. Tonight she had given the cold shoulder to every man in the honky-tonk.

He slowed and parked in front of the house. In the next block he saw a man stumbling along the sidewalk until he turned and disappeared inside a house.

Olivia's car approached and turned into her drive that was no more than a gravel path. When she stepped out of the car, she picked up a grocery sack and walked toward her house, merely glancing at him when he emerged from his car.

"We've talked," she said when he caught up with her. She brushed past him and climbed rickety steps, crossing the porch to unlock her door. Matt followed and held the screen door. He stood close enough to get a strong whiff of the odor of cigarette smoke trapped in her hair.

She looked up at him. "You're not welcome here. I've said all I need to say to you."

"Listen. You're carrying a Ransome. I want to help you and you damned well need support. Stop being so stubborn and listen to what I have to offer. For all you know, you could be turning down a million bucks."

Her eyebrows arched. "Am I?" she asked, startling him at her change in temperament because he thought he heard amusement in her voice.

"Let's go inside and talk," he answered. She gave him a level look and he wondered if she was going to send him on his way, but she shrugged and entered her house, leaving the door open behind her.

He followed her into a small, frame house that had to be nearly a hundred years old. White paint had peeled from the cracked walls, revealing a coat of dark blue paint. The furniture was threadbare and looked older than he was, yet there were some green plants and a few touches that contrasted with the dilapidation.

She tossed her purse on the sofa, set down the sack of groceries and motioned to him. "Have a seat."

"How long have you lived here?" he asked, looking around and sitting on an overstuffed chair covered in a faded, flowered slipcover. A blanket was thrown over the sofa and he suspected it hid holes.

"Almost a year now."

Leaning forward, he rested his elbows on his knees while he watched her kick off her shoes and rub her foot.

"I know you're going to school. You don't have any family. You work in a dive and you reek of cigarette smoke. The bar can't be healthy for your baby or you."

"I'm trying to get another job that pays at least as much as the one I have. I don't have the skills or the wardrobe for an office job," she said, thrusting out her chin defiantly. "Pay is higher at Two-Steppin' Ribs because the bar is out in nowhere."

"How many hours are you taking this semester?"

"Two classes—six hours. I'm in pre-law."

"You're a sophomore, aren't you?"

"I think you already know the answer. And you're thinking that a sophomore is not much for someone who is twenty-two, but it's the best I could do," she replied, curling her long legs beneath her and settling in the corner of the sofa. His gaze slid along her legs. He tried to keep his thoughts on his mission, but he was responding to her physically in a manner that shocked him.

"All right. Here's the deal," he said. "I'll send you to school. You quit that job and move out to the ranch with me—"

"No way! I'm sure you think I'm easy, but I'm not climbing into bed with you to get my tuition," she said, flinging the words at him and standing.

"Sit down," he said with such ice and authority that she did. "I don't want your body." Even as he said the words, a devilish urge made him too aware that he was lying to her as far as what his body desired. Yet he could control himself and good sense kept telling him that he shouldn't want her physically. She would be pure poison. He didn't want to get involved emotionally with any woman.

"I'll pay for your school, let you quit that damn job," he repeated, "take care of you and the baby. I'll pay your medical bills—"

"No one is that filled with benevolence. What do you want out of this generous offer?" she asked in a cynical voice.

"Stop fighting me," he said, gazing steadily into her green eyes and thinking that every inch of her made a man think of sex. "I want to know my niece or nephew. I want to make sure this baby is taken care of in the manner he or she should be. I don't want your body," he reaffirmed, trying to avoid looking at her lush body and failing annoyingly to stop thinking about it. "I want to know your baby. I want to see you able to take care of yourself and the baby. I can pay for your education. In turn, this Ransome will become part of our family. Dad has had one heart attack already. I want him to know his only grandchild."

"If you want your father to have a grandchild so badly, you should rethink your stance against marriage."

"I married once and never again for me," Matt replied grimly, refusing to discuss the matter further.

"What happened? She didn't like your bossy arrogance?"

He banked his irritation and ignored her question: "Your baby will be the only Ransome in the next generation. My dad isn't getting any younger and he desperately wants a grandchild. I think he's given up on all of us, but now, with your baby, his hopes are rekindled."

As Olivia bit her lip, Matt couldn't resist looking at her mouth.

"Look, dammit. What are you holding onto here besides your independence?" he asked. "This isn't a castle. Your job is tough and tiring and pays little. You work in an unhealthy atmosphere. Men hit on you, and I can imagine what they're saying to you—"

"And you won't hit on me?" she asked in a sarcastic tone.

"No, I won't," he said flatly, trying in vain to shove erotic images of her out of his mind. "You know you're an attractive woman, but you're like a relative," he said, while an inner voice laughed and he wiped his perspiring brow. When had the temperature in the small room climbed so high?

"What do you want?" she asked. "You look like the straight-arrow, determined, accustomed to getting-your-way type."

"I want to take care of my dad and our ranches—we own three. No commitments beyond my family and our ranches. I want my dad to get to know his only grandchild. Pretty damn simple," Matt snapped, thinking it should not be complicated, but it was. He was playing with dynamite right now by bringing her into their family.

"I suspect there's more to it than my baby."

"I swear I'm telling you the truth."

"I know I work in a bad place and I'm looking for another job," she said, waving her slender fingers at him. "I'm holding on to my independence because that's all I really have. I don't want to have to depend on you and I don't want to have to repay you for favors."

"If it reassures you, we can put my offer in a contract. I don't want anything physical," he repeated. "I'll pay for your school and all your expenses and your baby's. I'll pay you a lump sum up front so you're not beholden to me for money. You don't have to repay any of it."

"That sounds too generous. I know you can't understand someone holding such a value on independence, but it's important to me. In spite of what you say, I can't believe there aren't strings attached to your offer."

"Listen. I'm trying to give you the help you need to become

completely independent. In exchange, I want to know my brother's child That's all there is to it."

She glowered and inhaled, and he looked down as her full breasts strained against the fabric. When he glanced up, she frowned.

"It's difficult to be convinced that you really want to know this baby—or that your father wants a grandchild badly—when Jeff so totally denied us and was emphatic he didn't want anything to do with my baby."

"None of us knew Jeff's attitude. My guess is, his reaction was to get out of his responsibility, which was typical of my younger brother."

"So what happens later when I want to move on?"

"We'll work that out when we come to it. I hope you'll stick around until you finish your education. Maybe by then you'll like us and trust us enough to stay close permanently. Do you have long-term plans?"

"I intend to finish school and get a job. I still say, you could marry again if you want kids so all-fired much."

"There is already a baby coming who is a Ransome. I'm not going to turn my back on a child who has Ransome blood. I have to keep reminding you—your baby is my relative."

Matt stared at her while she glared at him and the clash of wills was tense, but along with the contention was a sexual undercurrent of desire. Sparks danced between them, and Matt was certain she felt the same attraction he did.

Instinctively, he knew the appeal was as unwanted to her as it was to him. Trying to control his insistent lust, he made a stronger effort to think only of the future and a baby he wasn't going to surrender without the fight of his life.

"If I give you a sum of cash up front and promise to pay your expenses, you won't feel dependent on me. I'll repeat—we can sign a contract."

"I don't want to get involved with Jeff's kin," she insisted and he wondered if she had a clue how much he was willing to give her to change her grim conditions.

"Possibly my offer will help with your decision. We'll set up a trust fund for your baby. I'll cover your expenses and you'll have room and board at the ranch. Plus how's a hundred thousand dollars paid to you, half now, half in six months?"

Two

Olivia stared in disbelief at Matt Ransome as the princely sum stunned her.

"For that much money, you want me, body and soul, plus my baby," she replied curtly as she stood. "Get out!"

"Sit down," he ordered in the cold, quiet voice he had used before that sent a chill down her spine, yet made her feel that the last notion on his mind was her body. She sat.

"I keep telling you that I can have our attorney draw up a contract. If you want, you can meet my family and talk to them."

Barely considering his family, Olivia nodded stiffly while the amount of money spun in her thoughts. The sum dazzled her. Unable to stop herself, she speculated about the classes she could take, the freedom she could have, the dreadful job that she could leave. It was more money than she could ever earn at the bar. Her heart pounded, her palms had grown damp and it was an effort to resist accepting his offer blindly and instantly. She realized silence was stretching between them and he was waiting patiently.

"You're very different from your brother," she remarked.

"I hope to hell I am," he said.

She had seen Matt Ransome at the rib place hours before he had spoken to her. She had never met him, but she had seen him once when she was with Jeff and he had told her that Matt was his brother. Matt had none of Jeff's easy charm or happy-go-lucky ways. He was perhaps a couple of inches shorter, more broad-shouldered, handsome in his own way with the same dark blue eyes and thick lashes. Matt's hair was black. Jeff's had been brown.

That first moment of a close encounter with Matt Ransome had disturbed her. She had to admit that she'd had a physical reaction to him that she'd never had with Jeff or any other man. She didn't know why, either, because Matt Ransome was too forceful, too determined to get his way to suit her. He was all business, but that first moment of looking directly into his blue eyes while he gazed back at her, had taken her breath, held her totally and had steamed with sexual tension. For a few seconds, she was certain that he had been locked into the same jolting awareness that she was.

Now here was his proposition that she still found difficult to believe from a man who disturbed her physically in a way no other man ever had. With most men, she had always felt in control. But Matt Ransome demolished that sense of power. She didn't like to acknowledge it, but she had to admit to herself that she was drawn to Matt in a purely physical way. She couldn't explain why and she didn't want to be. She never again wanted to be involved with a Ransome.

At the same time, Matt's offer was tempting beyond belief, but she wasn't rushing into an agreement. She had given her trust to Jeff and he had trampled it.

She cocked her head to one side to study Matt. "You know for the money you're offering, you could adopt a child."

"Since this baby is a Ransome, I intend to take care of it and I want to get to know him or her. Do you know what you're having?"

"It's too early. I haven't decided whether I want to know or not."

"We'll say a prayer for a girl. The males in this family haven't turned out so good."

"I'll think about your offer," she said coldly, standing. "It's time for you to go."

He stood. "Look, you can mull it over, but you know you need what I'm offering. In the meantime, you should move out of this neighborhood. Come stay at the ranch tonight."

"Tonight?" Again, he startled her. "I can't possibly—"

"Of course you can," he persisted. "I'll bet you don't have more than two suitcases of stuff. Do you rent this furnished or is this your furniture?"

"I rented it furnished. Look, if you're taking charge of my life, then that settles it, I'm not going," she said, hoping her voice was forceful and trying to keep her gaze from roaming down his long legs or across his broad chest.

"I'm trying to improve your situation," he stated patiently. "What's holding you in this place?"

Her face grew hot and she glanced away, unable to meet his direct gaze. "Nothing," she admitted. "Except you're a stranger."

"Not a total stranger. You knew Jeff, so you know a lot about me. You're not safe here. This isn't a healthy place for an expectant woman. You don't need to be alone and you could be a hell of a lot more comfortable. All right?"

Annoyed, she shook her head. "You're taking charge. Back off and give me some room. I'll think it over. I'll come out in the morning and we can discuss your offer more."

He inhaled and looked as if he were trying to cling to what little patience he had. "All right, but resign and get away from the secondhand smoke. At least think of your baby."

"I do think of my baby."

"If you'll get a pencil and paper, I'll give you directions to the ranch."

She glared at him and knew he held his annoyance in check. She didn't like him taking over, yet it was for the best. If she moved to the ranch, she knew she would be making a commitment from which it might be difficult to shake free.

She didn't like Matt's forceful ways. Maybe that's why Jeff had had such a rebellious nature.

"I'm beginning to understand why your brother was like he was."

Anger flashed in Matt's blue eyes. "My youngest brother wouldn't take responsibility for anything."

She realized she had touched a nerve. Dropping remarks about Jeff, she hurried to get a pen and paper. As Matt wrote directions to his ranch, she looked at his well-shaped hands, his thick, slightly curly eyelashes and straight nose. A faint dark stubble showed on his jaw.

"After knowing Jeff, who could not be relied on, I find it difficult to trust you," she admitted.

"I'll keep reminding you, I'm not like Jeff," Matt replied quietly. They stood only inches apart and he had focused on her with that intensity he had the first time they had made eye contact. Her insides got butterflies and her gaze lowered to his mouth while she wondered what it would be like to kiss him.

When she looked up to find him gazing at her mouth, her heart missed a beat. She drew herself up. "I want one point clear—you're a take-charge person. If I move to your ranch, you agree now that you won't try to run my life."

"I wouldn't think of it," he answered with sarcasm as the fiery clash of wills continued to snap between them. "But I am going to speak up when you do things that might endanger the health of your baby."

"Right now, you can forget about ever trying to take my baby from me."

"I know a child needs its mother. I don't want to jeopardize that relationship as long as you are a loving mother. Your family has a history of neglect and abuse."

"I'm not like my parents," she snapped while anger made her hot. "My folks drank, were into drugs. They were verbally abusive. They neglected me as well as themselves and were irresponsible and it killed them. I couldn't wait to get away from them," she said flatly. She studied him for a moment. "You know a lot about me. Especially for having just met me. More than Jeff knew, I think. How'd you find out so much?"

"I wanted to know about you before I started dealing with you. I hired a P.I. to check into your life."

Her displeasure heightened that he would have her background checked, but then she knew if she were making the offer he was, she might do the same.

"You don't approve, do you?" he asked.

"No, but I can understand why you wanted to know about my past. I'll think about your offer to move into your home," she said, knowing she should accept eagerly, but she was loath to relinquish her independence.

"We won't get in each other's way. It's a big house. Also, fall enrollment is open at the university in Fort Worth." He reached into a back pocket and withdrew brochures and a catalogue. "Here, you can look at these," he said and placed them on a table. "You can become a full-time student and graduate sooner," he said.

"You've been planning this for a while. How far from Fort Worth is your ranch? I've forgotten what Jeff told me."

"Thirty miles. Not far. You can commute easily."

They stared at each other, and she wondered if he intended doing what he said. She had been surprised by men before, so if Matt Ransome didn't live up to his part of their bargain, she could deal with it. She knew he lusted after her. It showed in the way he looked at her, but his control was evident also. She had the feeling that he didn't like her at all. She suspected he didn't approve of much his younger brother had done or the women Jeff had known. Matt Ransome would have seemed like ice, real straight and arrogant, except for the smoldering looks he gave her. What astounded her was the effect he had on her. Since Jeff, she had been immune to men, but she wasn't immune to Matt. He made her pulse race, her breath catch. She didn't want to react that way to him and she knew he didn't want to respond to her, so whatever kind of chemistry there was brewing between them, it was unwanted and hopefully would evaporate.

ing with her and telling her the truth? Was his sole
t in the baby?

ope so," she said quietly, looking around at her few pos-
ns. She would be glad to leave this house. It would take less
a couple of hours for her to get all her possessions packed.
he switched on a bedroom light, looking at the nondescript
l and the dresser, a chest of drawers that didn't match and a
rn braided rug on the floor. As she got ready for bed, she thought
out Jeff Ransome. She had enrolled in a two-year college,
working in a café until she had gotten the job at the Two-Steppin'
Ribs. It paid more so she put up with the smoke and the leering
men, but from the start, Jeff had been different from the others.

Tall, brown-haired and handsome, Jeff had gone to the Ribs
to gamble. There was a high-stakes poker game in a back room
that was invitation only and the night she'd met him, Jeff had
been part of it. After closing he had hung around and asked her
to go out with him.

Since she was twelve years old, she had known that she attracted males. Early on, she had learned to try to keep a wall
around herself, but when she met Jeff Ransome, he had
charmed his way past her defenses. She had been unable to
resist his charismatic personality.

As Olivia pulled on cotton pajamas, gathered up the school
catalog and brochure and climbed into bed, her thoughts went
back to Jeff. He'd been the second man in her life, which she
knew he hadn't believed. She'd had a wonderful time with him
until she discovered she was pregnant. They had used birth
control, but she had gotten pregnant anyway.

From that moment on, Jeff was through. And then a month
ago he had left for a trek in the rugged Himalaya mountains
where, in a daredevil climb, he'd had a fatal fall.

Olivia gazed into space, mulling over Matt Ransome's offer.
She had to accept, but as much as possible, she wanted it on
her terms, not his.

She opened the catalog and turned to the section on pre-
law, her major, and for the first time allowed herself to

"Are we finished for tonight?" she a
of her house.

"I don't think you're safe here. Anyone
into this place can do so easily if they have an
you want me to stay here? I can sleep in a chair

She smiled, amused by his offer of protection
no thanks. I've been taking care of myself for a lo
dad died five years ago. My mother died two year
I've taken care of both of them since I was twelve y
We lived in a lot tougher neighborhoods than this. Tha
reason I moved here. Cheap rent and a better area, althoug
sure it doesn't look suitable to you. One more night her
nothing to worry about."

He stared at her and she wondered if he was going to ins
she let him stay. It was obvious that he disapproved of her.
probably thought she was easy. If he got to know her, he wou
find out he was wrong in that judgment. The last thing sh
wanted was to be a live-in girlfriend, going from one brothe
to the other.

As they gazed at each other, that searing awareness flashed
between them. In spite of all her intentions to keep a wall
between them, it was impossible to resist reacting to Matt.
Right now her heart raced. Perspiration had broken out on his
forehead, and he seemed as riveted as she was.

Inhaling deeply, he spun away to cross the room to the door.
She trailed after him, pausing a few feet from him. "I gave you
my cell number. Call me if you need anything," he said.

"Thanks," she replied.

"Don't worry. You'll be glad if you say yes," he said. He
opened the door and strode outside. She followed, watching
Matt Ransome climb into his car and drive away.

When she stepped back inside, she looked around the shabby
room. By accepting Matt's offer, she could take care of her
baby, get her education, live in a safer place. She was scared
to celebrate because she hadn't been to the ranch yet, nor had
she spent a night under the same roof with Matt Ransome. Was

think of the windfall Matt Ransome was providing. If only it was exactly as he said and there were no hidden agendas, no strings attached and no unpleasant surprises ahead for her. She could move to the Ransome ranch and quit her job! In the early hours of morning, the whole offer seemed surreal, and she suspected that as soon as she settled on the ranch, Matt would want to sleep with her. He was appealing, sexy and generated sparks in her the way no other man had.

Forget it, she told herself, knowing she would not go from one brother to another. "If I accept his offer, I vow I won't have sex with Matt Ransome," she said aloud, trying to stop remembering the tingles she had when she gazed into Matt's blue eyes.

Forcing her thoughts off Matt, she wondered about her future and his offer. Was there anything she could do to get Matt's proposition more on her own terms?

The next morning her palms were damp from nervousness as she drove through an open gate and passed a sign announcing the Ransome ranch. In minutes she turned a bend in the ranch road. Ahead spread houses, a barn, a corral, pens and outbuildings. A pumping windmill stood near a stock tank filled with water.

When she drew closer, she looked at an intimidating, sprawling stone ranch house with a shake shingle roof. It was surrounded by immaculate, lush green lawns and a profusion of flowers in well-tended beds that all proclaimed the wealth of the owner. She had never lived in a house that looked as grand as this one. Swallowing hard, Olivia couldn't imagine herself suddenly part of the Ransome family.

A rail fence enclosed the yard and two live oaks gave inviting shade that failed to calm Olivia's nerves. On the porch the hanging pots of yellow bougainvillea, scarlet gaillardia and purple impatiens added a dreamlike feeling. This could be her new home. She couldn't fathom it.

Adding to her jittery nerves and disbelief, Matt Ransome came striding outside. In a white T-shirt, jeans and western boots, he looked muscled, tough and electrifying. Without saying a word he created a high voltage magnetism. The sight of him did nothing to calm her nerves.

He motioned her where to park in front of a six-car garage. When she climbed out, she was conscious of her cutoffs and her white T-shirt.

"Hi there," Matt said in a deep voice as he took a box from her car. In his T-shirt that revealed sculpted muscles and his tight jeans, his sensuality jumped a notch. One look in his eyes confirmed that the sexual appeal between them burned as hot as ever. When she stepped out, she looked up to see him gazing at her waist.

"You don't look pregnant," he said.

An inner voice told her to keep everything impersonal with Matt, but she couldn't do what she knew she should. "I guess it's because I'm tall," she replied breathlessly, mindful of how close he stood. She barely knew what she said to him. He should move away. She should step aside. Instead, she gazed up at him while her heartbeat continued to accelerate.

Silence between them carried sparks. When his attention lowered to her mouth, her pulse drummed. As he gazed at her, the blatant, scalding desire in his eyes heated her.

"No physical relationship comes with this package," she repeated.

"It damn well doesn't," he replied, sounding half angry. "I don't ever want to get involved again except in the most superficial manner. You and I absolutely don't need entanglement between us."

"That's something we can agree on. It would help if you'd move away."

Something flickered in the depths of his eyes before he leaned around her to pick up another one of her boxes.

"I'll get your things and then I'll show you around. Have you quit your job?"

"No, I haven't. I figured whatever we decide to do, I'll work tonight."

Matt straightened up and she saw the hard look back in his features. He shook his head. "You quit today. You don't owe them anything and you shouldn't be there one more hour."

"I thought you weren't going to meddle in my life," she said, trying to curb her temper.

"Where the baby is concerned, I'll interfere. That nightclub isn't healthy. They'll manage without you."

"Look—"

"No, you look," he said quietly. "The bar's atmosphere isn't healthy. They're going to get along without you. If we have a deal, part of it includes you taking care of yourself and your unborn baby."

Where sexual tension had spun tightly between them only moments ago, now friction set sparks flying. She glared at him, yet she suspected she would get nowhere if she argued the rest of the day.

"Why do you want to wait tables so all-fired badly?" Matt asked her.

"I don't. That isn't it."

"There you are."

She put her hands on her hips. "I'm here tentatively. We haven't agreed on what we're going to do. I haven't accepted your offer. We need to discuss it before you start taking complete charge."

"Let me show you around, let you select your room and then we'll sit down and see if we can't come to terms," he said, lifting the last box and putting it under his arm. "Tomorrow I'll introduce you to everyone who works here. Mrs. Marley is the housekeeper and cook. You'll meet her at the end of the week. She's here two days a week. Fridays, she cooks. Saturdays, she cleans. My dad lives down the road from me. She's at his house Monday through Thursday."

Olivia nodded.

"Wait a minute," Matt said and set a box on her car. Following Matt's gaze, she watched a tall, sandy-haired man approach and shake hands with Matt.

"Olivia, this is our foreman, Sandy McDermott," Matt said easily. "Sandy, meet Olivia Brennan who will be staying with us a while."

"I'm glad to meet you, Sandy," she said, extending her hand and smiling.

"Happy to meet you, Miss Brennan. Glad to have you here."

"It's Olivia, Sandy. Call me Olivia."

Sandy nodded. "Nice meeting you, Olivia," he said, turning to talk to Matt. Olivia listened while they discussed cattle and a world she didn't know. Matt was quick and decisive and more relaxed than when he was dealing with her. As soon as Sandy told them goodbye and left, she and Matt headed for the house.

She was aware of Matt walking close beside her. Her jittery nerves kept her on edge, and she wondered what she was getting herself into.

Once again Matt took her arm and she drew a deep breath. She hadn't known him twenty-four hours, yet his slightest touch set her ablaze. She couldn't fathom the chemistry. She had known other handsome, decisive males and she had had no trouble dealing with them and no difficulty ignoring them. Until now. Even Jeff with all his charm had never carried the electricity of a bolt of lightning the way Matt did.

She wondered again what she was getting into if she accepted Matt's offer that was a windfall in her circumstances. She was heartily glad to be out of the bar and away from lustful men. At the same time, she wanted this bargain to be partially on her terms. Her queasy nerves jangled when she thought about her plan and her requests. She had no idea how Matt would react. The knowledge was constantly with her that she was taking a risk by making her own demands because if she accepted his offer and he did what he said and kept his bargain, her life would improve beyond her wildest dreams.

He held the door, following her inside an enormous kitchen with oversize windows. Sunlight streamed into the room that held maple cabinetry, granite countertops, a marble floor and maple furniture. The floor-to-ceiling windows overlooked a patio and a pool with sparkling blue water.

"This is beautiful," she said, unable to keep a breathless tone of awe out of her voice. "It doesn't look like what I imagined."

"Jeff and I must have created the wrong impression."

Her gaze flew to him and heat flooded her cheeks. Embarrassed by her reaction, she bit her lip.

"You probably thought we lived in a cabin with mounted heads and gun racks and the sort."

"No," she denied halfheartedly and then shrugged. "Maybe something like that," she admitted.

"C'mon. Let me show you this wing of the house." He took her arm lightly, yet the contact sizzled, and as they crossed the kitchen, her surroundings paled in comparison to the man beside her.

From the hall he led her into a family room and her awe returned at the sight of a twenty-foot-high cathedral ceiling, a massive stone fireplace, luxurious tan leather furniture and pictures of landscapes.

"This is a dream!" she gasped and her face flushed. "You can tell I've never lived in a house like this," she said.

"Well, now you do," he said. "It's comfortable. Across the hall are the living and dining rooms," he said, taking her arm again as they returned to the hall. "On the other side of the kitchen is a utility room, exercise room and my office. The bedrooms are in the opposite wing. Other than my bedroom, in the southeast end of the house, you can have whichever bedroom you want."

As he led her through a workout room, a media room and his office, the elegant furnishings overwhelmed Olivia. It was a dream-come-true moment to think she would live in this palace. She realized Jeff and Matt weren't the ordinary cowboys she had imagined they were. The house reeked of money and power and she wondered whether she could hold her own and govern her baby's future against the Ransomes' wishes.

"We'll have a decorator help you with the nursery." Matt's words jolted her back into awareness of the moment.

"I won't be here forever." Olivia gave him a startled, wide-eyed look.

"That's all right. You'll return to visit and bring the baby."

"You're so certain!" she exclaimed, yet now she realized part of the source of his arrogance and assurance. Growing up in a home like this, how could he be anything except confident?

"Shouldn't I be?" he asked, looking blandly at her.

Olivia stopped to face him, a frown creasing her brow. "Our lives are so different."

"It doesn't matter, Olivia," he replied easily. "We'll be related to the baby and we'll want to see him or her through the years. It'll save you money to live here until you finish your education."

She merely nodded and returned to thinking about her future while she looked at more rooms in a house that dazzled her.

"How's this for you?" he asked later, leading the way into a bedroom that took her breath and she could not imagine living in it.

She stood in the room large enough to contain the house she rented. The room was plush beyond her wildest dreams. It was ample for a king-size bed with a bronze headboard, a massive mahogany chest, bookshelves, a wide-screen television, a maroon sofa, a rocking chair and assorted tables. The decor was maroon with accents of white and beige and an oriental rug partially covering the gleaming plank floor.

She knew she wasn't hiding her amazement. She reminded herself that it was premature to celebrate her newfound fortune, her future prospects or this house that could possibly become her home. In the next few minutes, she knew, it could all disappear from her life as swiftly as it had entered.

The time had come to present her conditions.

"This is beyond anything I had imagined," she said softly, turning to face him. Her pulse drummed. She wanted to learn how earnest he really was about this whole proposition. "Shall we discuss our future and terms of a contract?" she asked, the words *our future* causing her insides to clench.

"Sure," he replied, giving her a long, speculative look that made her feel he knew her every thought. "Let's get a drink and sit in the family room."

They walked in silence back to the kitchen and she watched, barely aware of what he was doing while her pulse beat faster and her nervousness increased. At the last minute she vacillated between an overwhelming desire to accept his offer unconditionally and reap the fortune, or risk her demands that would either cause him to send her packing or solidify her prospects and fortune.

Finally, they were seated in the family room at a polished oak game table with tall, frosted glasses of ice and lemonade and a plate of cookies in front of them. She couldn't eat or drink anything. Aware that her entire prospects hung in the balance, she inhaled deeply to calm down.

"You've had time to think it over. You're here on the ranch. Does this mean you'll accept my offer?" he asked.

His blue eyes cut into her like shards of a glacier. He was formidable and determined, but she clung to her course. It was time to see how much he would commit to what he wanted. She took a deep breath and raised her chin while she locked her hands together.

"You're being very generous," she said, still awed by his offer and filled with trepidation over what she was about to demand from him for her part. "I have a counteroffer to make to you."

Fire flashed in the depths of his eyes and a muscle worked in his jaw. She suspected he was bracing for her to ask for more money.

"All right. Name your conditions and price," he said, grinding out the words. "How much Ransome money do you want?"

"You've made an overwhelmingly generous offer, but if you're truly committed to protecting this baby and raising it as a Ransome, then I want you to give my baby the Ransome name. I want a paper marriage, an in-name-only marriage that we can later dissolve." Her heart thundered so loudly that she could barely hear herself speak. "In other words, will you marry me?"

Three

Stunned, Matt stared at her. "You want me to marry you?" he repeated in amazement.

"Yes, if you're so determined to make my baby a part of your family. It'll be the same conditions you've already given me, plus marriage. This way, you're more committed. My child will legitimately be a Ransome as it should have been all along. You'll do the honorable thing that your brother would not do."

Matt stared at her. Anger and shock rocked him that she would put one more demand on him when he had given her an offer that was magnanimous beyond anything she had ever known in her life. Then he noticed her white knuckles and her hands doubled into fists. Perspiration dotted her brow and worry glazed her green eyes.

Suddenly he could see her viewpoint and why she wanted legitimacy. In the future marriage would truly tie Jeff's child into the family.

Yet it would bind Matt to Olivia in a manner he never intended. For an instant heat flashed in him at the thought of marriage to her. On a purely physical level he speculated about her shapely, naked body in his arms. With lightning speed the image aroused him.

He forced his thoughts back to business and a contract with her and a paper marriage. A marriage in name only.

"We can dissolve it as soon as I get my law degree," she added.

Could he stay under the same roof with her and keep his hands to himself? He had planned to do just that before she had come up with the proposal.

"You want it all," he said quietly, and she flushed, her cheeks turning a bright pink.

"No. I don't want sex with you," she answered bluntly. "You know it wouldn't be a true marriage. Not in any manner. But you can see that if you really want what you've been telling me, it would give my baby more protection and give me a better deal."

"Hell, yes," he snapped. "You could sue me for divorce and half of everything I own."

"You said we'd have a contract. We'll have a prenuptial agreement that will list terms as both of us want them. You can have your lawyer draw it up."

Matt was impressed. She was taking charge of part of their bargain, making some shrewd demands and she once again surprised him. He rubbed the back of his head. She had him in a corner and she knew it. He didn't want to marry her, not even a fake, paper marriage of convenience because that would be legally binding.

But if he backed out on marriage, she might refuse his deal and the baby would go out of the Ransome family.

"And you still want all the rest I've offered—the education, the cash, the trust fund for the baby?"

"I want the education and the trust fund. I'd like some cash so I can go to school full time, but if I live at the Ransome ranch, I think you could cut the amount of money in half or even less if you want. As soon as I finish my education, we can dissolve the union. I don't intend for it to be permanent."

"I've got to think about it. I hadn't planned on marriage," he said and watched her let out her breath and unclench her hands. She raised her chin.

"I didn't think you'd do it." She stood and sighed. "You were better than your brother, but it's not good enough. Since you're not interested in my terms, I'll keep my independence and move on."

"You'll be walking out on a fabulous future that's a whole hell of a lot better than you're doing now or can do. You're selling your baby short by turning down my offer."

"Perhaps, but I'm not the one who wants something here," she said. "If you're willing to commit to this baby, I want the whole deal—I want support and legitimacy and some of the things your brother should have given me." She shrugged. "I'm accustomed to tough times. You can take it or leave it."

He gazed into green eyes that were fiery and unyielding and he was certain she wasn't bluffing about turning down his offer. He believed every word she said and it increased his anger that she was being so foolish, yet at the same time, he couldn't keep from appreciating her determination to get more for her child. And deep down, Matt knew she was right. He might have done the same thing himself, had he been in her place.

"Sit down," he ordered quietly, his anger growing. "I didn't say I wouldn't do it. I simply want to think about it like you wanted to consider my offer last night."

She sat and he stared hard at her. She stared right back at him and he felt tension coil.

"I'll talk to my attorney about it," Matt finally replied, buying some time before he made any kind of commitment. "In the meantime, call and quit your job and settle in. I'll introduce you to people who live and work on the ranch."

"Until you come to a decision, I'm not leaving a job that pays better than most around here. I'm going to my room to get ready to go to work."

Matt stood and watched her walk away. He wanted to grab her and shake her and he had never felt that way with a woman before. Not even Margo before she walked out on him. Olivia Brennan got to him as no one ever had.

What was worse, was that steady, fiery sexual awareness of her, a hot attraction that kept his nerves on edge. Marry her!

His whole being wanted to yell never, but then he thought about what he would be tossing aside. He was certain she would walk right out of his life and at any point in time, she could move far from Texas. She had no roots, no ties except going to college and right now she was between semesters. Right now, she could move away without much disruption in her life. Her college credits would transfer.

"Dammit!" He pushed back his chair with a scrape and crossed the room to call the family attorney.

He presented the problem swiftly, asking questions about a prenuptial agreement, keeping his eye on the clock. While part of him listened to the lawyer speaking, part of Matt's attention was focused on hearing Olivia return.

Matt finally replaced the receiver and stared at the phone. As he suspected, marriage, even a paper-only union, would be far more binding than the bargain Matt had intended to strike with Olivia. But it could be dissolved, and he could put stipulations to try to protect himself from later demands. It didn't mean she wouldn't sue or take him to court and he would have to fight her later. On the other hand, the baby would legally be a Ransome.

Matt rubbed the back of his neck and swore under his breath. He didn't want to get bound to her. Not Olivia or any other woman.

He heard her in the hall and he crossed the family room in quick long strides. In the kitchen he caught up with her and she glanced at him as he strode into the room.

"Wait a minute!" he snapped.

Her brows lifted in question as he crossed the room to stand with only inches separating them. "I called our attorney and talked to him," Matt declared. "Marriage is a hell of a lot more commitment than you're asking me to make."

"You are the one who wants my baby in your family, re-member?"

"I'm considering what you want. Call in sick tonight. You can miss one night and still keep your job."

"I can, but I don't see any reason to. I'm going to work. I need every dollar I can earn."

"I've offered you a damn good deal."

"Indeed, you have, but I told you that I want it all," she said softly. She had on her tight red T-shirt and short cutoffs.

"Hell, I'll pay your salary for tonight, but you take sick leave," he ordered, annoyed that she was uncooperative. He was as angered by her demands and stubborn will as he was by his own heated response to her.

She stared at him a moment and he thought she was going to still refuse. Instead, she nodded and crossed the room to the phone, hanging her red vinyl purse on a hook by the door.

She asked for another woman and spoke softly, turning her back to Matt, but he heard her tell her friend that something had come up and she wouldn't be there tonight.

"You could have told her you were sick," Matt said as soon as she replaced the receiver and turned around.

"I'm not sick. Kira will think of some excuse for me, no doubt. I don't think you have a very high opinion of me," she remarked. "I'm sure you think I'm cheap and easy and not too bright."

"I'll admit that I might have thought that at one time, but the P.I.'s report changed my opinion. You don't have any men in your life now. Your grades are top-notch. My opinion of you changes almost hourly. You constantly surprise me."

"The same as you astound me. So did your brother. To my misfortune, I misjudged him in too many ways. I'll never trust a Ransome again like I did Jeff."

"You want to marry a Ransome," Matt reminded her.

"That is purely a business arrangement for both of us." She took her purse off the hook. "I'm going to unpack my things, shower and change before you show me around. I'd just as soon not meet people dressed like this."

He nodded and watched her start out of the room. At the door she turned back to look at him. "Unlike Jeff Ransome, you can trust me. If I give you my word, I'll keep it." She left, and he heard the soft slap of her sneakers in the hall.

"I'll be in my office," he called after her and headed down the hall, wanting to talk to his attorney again.

Olivia closed the door to her new bedroom, walking around the room and touching the furniture lightly. She shook from pent-up nerves and her proposal to Matt Ransome. To demand that the man who owned this mansion marry her—it took her breath with its presumptuousness. How could she be that brash and calculating? Yet it would give the world to her baby.

Her proposal of marriage had jarred Matt. It wasn't what he had expected or wanted, yet he was considering it. She could detect a grudging respect growing in him.

She paused in front of an elegant rosewood-framed mirror and looked at herself. Her riot of red hair always gave the impression of a wanton woman. Her breasts were full, adding to the attraction to males. She ought to cut her hair and buy fake glasses. With the money—if she made a deal with Matt—she would be able to afford to get her hair fixed and buy new clothes.

She frowned at her image. She shouldn't think about where or how she would spend one nickel of his money. She didn't have a deal yet with Matt, and they might not ever have one.

With her proposal, had she opened it up for Matt to take control of her child? That question nagged at her. If they married, he would legally have rights and she was certain he would have all sorts of opinions on how Jeff's baby should be raised and what schools it should attend. Never would she be able to pack, divorce Matt and walk away as easily as she would if she simply accepted Matt's money offer.

At the thought of relinquishing control of all decisions concerning her child, her stomach knotted. On the other hand, giving her baby the Ransome name and making him or her an heir would offset letting Matt into their lives. And from what she could see, Matt seemed to truly want what was best for her child.

She had never had a decent home life. She glanced around

the splendid bedroom and knew she would be giving her offspring the best.

And Matt? How long could they resist the sizzling physical attraction? She didn't want to ever love another Ransome, another untrustworthy male and in this case, an arrogant, controlling one. Yet even now when Matt was away from her, she was hot and breathless merely thinking about him. It was a volatile chemistry she didn't have with other men and it might make living under the same roof with him a challenge. Seduction was unwanted, but would she be strong enough to resist the attraction, she wondered.

Could she be uncompromising and walk away if he rejected her proposal?

She couldn't answer her own question. She thought of the money he offered, the chance for her to get through school quickly, then care for herself and the baby. How could she walk away from all that? Would it be horribly unfair to her child to turn her back on Matt's offer?

Yet she suspected if she didn't walk away, he would never come back with acceptance of her proposal. And she wanted the Ransome name and all that went with it.

Her gaze drifted around the room again and the thought of her baby being part of the fortune of this family took her breath! She strolled to the window and looked out at grounds that were well tended. Beyond them acres of range land stretched to the horizon. The wealth of the place was so foreign to her, she might as well have been in another country. Would Matt consider running the risk of letting her lay claim to some of what he owned?

Matt wrote out a hasty prenuptial agreement, trying to think of all the things he wanted to put into the document so he would be prepared when he saw his attorney.

His mind kept jumping to Olivia, remembering watching her and touching her. He groaned and rubbed the back of his neck. He had known her less than twenty-four hours and he couldn't get her out of his mind.

Disgusted with himself that he couldn't stop thinking about her, Matt went to look in the desk in his bedroom for a copy of the prenuptial agreement he'd had with Margo. They had married young and both had come from wealthy families so they had drawn up a prenup agreement, but when they parted, there had been no hassle over money. With her tremendous salary and her family's money, she cared nothing about demands on Matt. She simply wanted out of the marriage to pursue her career.

In the hall Matt passed Olivia's closed door and thought about her in the shower, water pouring over that lush body and down her long legs. He groaned and walked faster, suspecting he should go work out and burn some energy. A whole evening with Olivia was going to be hellish temptation.

"Matt—"

He turned as she opened her door and stepped into the hall. Her shirt was pulled out of her cutoffs and partially unbuttoned, the open V giving a tantalizing glimpse of heart-stopping curves and cleavage.

"I can't get the hot water faucet to turn," she said. "Is it broken or am I doing something wrong? I can't imagine the plumbing breaking in this castle."

"Oh, hell. Sorry, I forgot. I've intended to get that fixed. And the plumbing does break on occasion," he added with amusement. "I'll get a wrench. It won't take more than a minute to repair it. Or you can move to any of the other occupied bedrooms."

"I'll wait if you don't mind repairing it."

He left to get pliers, a washer and a wrench and returned to her room, taking a deep breath before he went inside. She stood by the window, and he hoped she stayed out of the bathroom.

The scent of her perfume hung in the air and he tried to ignore it and think about water and pipes. As he leaned over the tub, working on the faucet, he swore because he hadn't taken care of the plumbing before she arrived or remembered it and put her in a different bedroom.

In minutes the faucet functioned again, and he picked up his wrench and pliers. As he started out, she entered the room and they almost collided. Taking her arm, he steadied her. "Sorry, Olivia," he said.

She looked up at him and again, he was ensnared in wide, thickly lashed green eyes. Desire rocked him and her eyes half-closed in a sultry expression that took his breath. He placed one hand on the doorjamb beside her and leaned closer. When she inhaled deeply, his gaze lowered and then returned to her full lips. Hemming her in, he could feel the heat from her voluptuous body, detect the come-hither fragrance she wore.

"We can find out now and get this out of the way between us," he said softly, leaning closer.

Her eyelids drooped a fraction as she slanted him a sensual look that set his pulse pounding. He slipped his arm around her waist and heard her gasp. She was soft, warm, all curves. He took his time, giving her a chance to pull away or protest or whatever she wanted.

Instead, when she placed her hand on his forearm and gazed up at him with a hot look, his body responded. If he was damned for it, he was going to kiss her.

With a seductive look from her, he was hard, wanting her, wanting to plunder her swollen lips, to taste and explore and see what a storm he could stir in her. Never had he seen a woman who looked more ready for sex.

Somewhere in the depths of his being, he knew he was crossing a line, going against what he had sworn he would avoid. With the temptation of a Pandora's box, he couldn't resist even if he knew in his heart that he was opening himself up for unending trouble.

As he leaned closer, she tilted her head up. Her breath was sweet and she was soft in the curve of his arm. His mouth came down on hers, opening her lips, his tongue sliding inside her mouth. Hot and wet, his kiss demanded more. He wanted to discover her sexually and his kiss and his body pressing hers was the fiery beginning.

She wrapped her arms around his neck, leaned into him,

molding her soft curves against him as she kissed him in return. Her tongue played over his, stroking and stirring his blinding need.

His rational thought had been lost back there when she first pressed against him. He tightened his arm around her, pulling her closer into his embrace, leaning over her and taking her searing kisses, letting go the pent-up longing he had controlled until now.

His pulse roared, drowning out other sounds, and he thought she would melt him with her scalding kisses. Why was she so different? he wondered. His heart thudded and he was in flames while below his belt he was rock-hard. He pulled her up tightly against him as his hand slid down her back and then trailed over the enticing curve of her bottom.

Her softness fanned the fire that consumed him. He ached to drown in her softness and unleash all her promised passion.

Grabbing a silky handful of her hair, he held her. When her hips twisted against him, he groaned.

Their kiss had escalated and spun out of control, seconds becoming minutes, time lost in need. She was too hot to handle, yet too desirable to release. Danger, danger ran through his thoughts, but he paid no heed. He never wanted to stop kissing her, kisses that were etched in his memory. Kisses that bound him to her in spite of all his reluctance.

Dimly, he became aware of her hands pressed on his chest, lightly pushing against him.

With an effort he opened his eyes, looking down at her to see her watching him. He released her and she stepped away, her gaze raking over him. "That was pure lust," she whispered.

"There was nothing pure about the past few minutes," he retorted, breathing heavily, seeing her gasp for breath as much as he did.

"I wasn't going to do that," she said, shooting him a torrid glance and then snapping her mouth closed.

"It's not going to happen again," he said, grinding out his words, hating his loss of control. His insides churned because emotionally, he hadn't wanted to kiss her. Physically, he lusted to have her in his bed with her naked body against him. "I don't think either one of us intended that kiss to happen, but it did and it seemed inevitable. Now it's over and done and we can forget about it," he said, wondering if he was trying to convince himself. In a lifetime, could he forget her kisses?

"That wasn't what I intended," she repeated in a low voice.

"There's some chemistry that we both gave in to, but it doesn't need to happen again."

She gave him a level, direct look. "So you're sorry you kissed me."

"You know I'm not, but we'll go back like we were."

When she nodded and closed the door, he let out his breath and shook his head. Why had he kissed her? Every shred of common sense told him to keep his hands to himself.

Burning with desire, he stormed down the hall. The fire in her kisses had been even more than he had expected. And his thoughts seethed about her marriage proposal and the prenuptial agreement, because now he felt differently about her demands and expectations.

Their relationship had just changed. Whether she knew it yet or not, his feelings toward her had intensified. How easily she could wreck his peaceful life! His reaction to Olivia was lust. Lust and anger and he needed to keep tight control of both emotions. He promised himself he would never let down his guard with her again. After Margo he would never trust a woman. Margo had taken his heart and stomped it to a million pieces. He didn't ever want to risk his heart with another woman.

He charged into his bedroom and slammed the door, crossing to his desk to open a drawer and once again get the prenuptial agreement from his marriage. Margo had made no demands on him. She had wanted out of the marriage and between her job and her family, she'd had all the money she could possibly want so there had been no problems there. The only problem had been that he had thought he was in love with her and he suspected she had only briefly been in love with him.

Looking at stipulations, he pored over the agreement some more and jotted notes while he wondered how many of his demands Olivia would accept.

Thinking about Olivia, he paused. She was honest, intelligent and shrewd. Had Jeff had a clue about what she was really like or had he simply seen her as a gorgeous, sexy woman?

Matt knew his brother well enough to know the answer to his question as swiftly as the question had risen—Jeff wouldn't get beyond sex.

Matt dropped his pen. He did not want to marry Olivia and damned if he would! After the poverty she had lived in, he couldn't imagine that she would walk away from the comfort and luxury he was offering.

While a plan formed in his mind, he stared out the window. He would give her two days of fabulous living—fly her to Houston, buy her a fancy wardrobe and shower her with jewelry and clothes she had never been able to afford. He would wine and dine her at places that would impress the most hardened sophisticate. Then see if she still wanted to reject his offer when he turned down her marriage proposal.

He picked up his phone to call and change his appointment with his lawyer. Next he called to get the Ransome corporate jet ready.

He strode down the hall and knocked on her door.

"Just a minute," she called. She swung the door open to face him. She stood with a towel wrapped around her and looking at her was as jolting as getting socked in the middle and having the wind knocked out of him.

Her slender shoulders were bare and the white towel was a contrast to her creamy skin. The towel was midthigh and all he could think about was only a towel covered her naked body.

While heat flashed through him, his heart thudded. He wanted to reach for her, remove that towel and pull her into his arms. Memories of her kisses fanned the flames that consumed him and for an instant, he was tongue-tied.

Her hair tumbled over her shoulders and she still had a few

drops of water that sparkled on one shoulder. She had been sexy in the T-shirt and cutoffs. In a towel, she was gorgeous.

He realized he was staring and she shifted impatiently. "Yes?" she asked, tilting her head.

"Get dressed," he said, hating the husky scrape in his voice. "I've made arrangements for a plane and I'll take you shopping in Houston so we can get you some new clothes. You'll need them. We'll eat there tonight and then we can fly back here or get rooms there."

"You're not doing this to postpone having to reach a decision about my proposal, are you?" she asked.

"Partially," he admitted, suspecting it wouldn't fool her if he gave her any other answer. "We're making big, life-changing decisions about our futures, though, so what will a twenty-four hour postponement hurt?"

"It might get me fired from my job if I don't show up two nights in a row."

"You can be back by tomorrow night," he answered.

She stared at him while she seemed to be mulling things over and finally she nodded. "I can be ready in ten minutes," she said and closed the door.

He stared at the closed door and still saw the image of her in the white towel. He wiped his brow. How was he going to cope with her under his roof for the next several years? He wanted the baby close, but if every encounter with Olivia was like the last two, he would be a basket case in no time.

Matt charged back to his room to call his favorite hotel and reserve adjoining suites. He made dinner reservations and then hurried to shower and shave and get dressed to go.

Ten minutes later he entered the family room to find her waiting. His gaze raked over her, taking in her denim skirt and simple, sleeveless white cotton blouse and sandals. He suspected what few clothes she owned were practical and cheap. There would be no way she could afford anything fancy or expensive unless she had the good fortune to find it in a secondhand shop.

Even so, the sight of her made his pulse accelerate and he

still had to fight the urge to want to touch her as he squelched images of her without the denim skirt or white blouse.

"I've never flown before," she said.

"Good! You'll like it," he answered, taking her arm and steering her out of the house and toward his car. He wanted to dazzle her and make her want to stay so badly that she would give up all thought of marriage.

They drove in silence to Meacham International Airport in Forth Worth. As they approached the waiting plane, her eyes were larger than usual. She was pale and silent, gazing with awe in her expression at the sleek jet awaiting them.

In a short time they were buckled into their comfortable seats with Olivia near a window. She seemed overwhelmed and he hoped her life was changing forever today and she would never want to go back to the poverty and hard life she had known in the past.

The moment they sped down the runway and then lifted into the air, she flashed him a brilliant smile that set his heart pounding. "This is fabulous!" she exclaimed, and satisfaction shot through him. Hopefully, in forty-eight hours he would be able to tell her no to marriage and she would cave in to his terms. All her awe and pleasure over the trip were only beginning— he could imagine how she would feel after two days of lavishly showering her with whatever she wanted. He smiled in return.

Four hours later, his satisfaction had increased. He swam laps in the hotel pool while he waited for Olivia who was getting her hair cut and styled. He had dinner reservations and after the first hour with her he had left her to shop on her own.

He glanced at his watch and climbed out of the pool to dress for dinner. She had seemed as overwhelmed by the hotel as she had been by their flight. Matt smiled grimly. He didn't want to deal with her about anything, but at least now it would be on his terms and not hers.

No one could live like this for two days and then go back to a grinding job at a rough Texas honky-tonk.

He dressed in a navy suit for dinner. He had helped her

select a simple black dress for dinner tonight, a dress with a price that had made her eyes grow round with wonder.

Matt knocked on the door of her suite and waited. The door swung open and Olivia smiled at him.

Once again, she stunned him and threw him off guard. Drawing a deep breath, Matt stared at her.

Four

"Good evening," Olivia said with far more assurance than she felt. At the sight of Matt, who was handsome, commanding and appealing in an immaculate white shirt and navy suit, her qualms faded momentarily to be replaced by a jump in her pulse.

Matt's gaze drifted over her in a thorough assessment that was as provocative as a caress. "You look sensational," he said softly.

"Thank you," she replied, knowing they were treading dangerous ground. She reminded herself that he was a Ransome with all the complications of being Jeff's brother. Her smile faded and she inhaled, fighting that irresistible draw she experienced around Matt.

In spite of her wariness, she couldn't keep from being pleased by the admiration in his expression. She was certain that his compliment had been sincere. Earlier, she had hardly known herself after the hairstylist finished. Her hair was cut, the sides brought up and looped on her head, the rest tumbling down her back. Instead of the simple black dress Matt had selected, she had found a dark blue one she liked that had a low-cut, draped back and was sleeveless with a skirt that stopped inches above her knees. She loved the cool silk lining that was smooth against her skin when she stepped into it.

"Ready to go?" he asked, and she nodded, picking up her purse.

"So is this a truce, more or less?" she asked as they headed to the elevators.

"Might as well be," he answered easily, yet she had a suspicion his animosity toward her had changed little. "You've moved into my house and we'll be together a lot from now on so we might as well get along."

She smiled disarmingly at him, yet she couldn't get rid of her suspicions that his sudden change in attitude hid an ulterior motive. Whether it did or not, she intended to enjoy the evening. She was with a handsome, sexy man, going to an elegant restaurant and she was dressed in the most gorgeous, expensive dress she had ever owned. Tonight she was Cinderella. She would enjoy herself until the clock struck twelve or whatever happened to burst her bubble.

Today, his kisses had rocked her. Remembering caused her lips to tingle. She hated that he had stirred feelings she thought were long dormant.

His kiss had plundered and all that pent-up desire that burned in the depth of his blue eyes had poured into his kiss and demolished any resistance she might have had. Tonight she would be even more susceptible to his charm.

As they left the hotel and climbed into a limousine, it came to her what he was possibly doing—giving her a taste of a lifestyle she had never known, but soon would be able to afford if she accepted his offer.

Anger flashed at the realization of his motive. Of course that was what he was doing! His smiles held all the threat of a crouching tiger. In his own way, Matt was fighting for what he wanted. Yet she couldn't blame him, because she was doing the same with her threat to walk if he didn't accept her terms.

They rode in the back of the limo across from each other and she smiled at him.

Desire blazed in his eyes, cutting across the battle between them. While she watched, he reached into his pocket. "I bought something for you today," he said, handing a small box to her.

Surprised, she glanced at the box and then at him. She was tempted to throw it at him for what he was doing, but then she reminded herself that he was trying to win her over to agreeing to his offer just as much as she intended to persuade him to consent to her proposal.

She opened the box. Nestled inside was a gold, diamond-studded bangle. Catching the light, the diamonds sparkled. "It's beautiful!" she gasped, momentarily forgetting his motive or her caution, because she had never dreamed of owning such a piece of jewelry.

He reached over to pick it up. Taking her hand in his warm, strong fingers, he slipped the bracelet on her slender wrist.

"Thank you! It's absolutely gorgeous!" she exclaimed, her emotions churning because all at once, she was both thrilled to receive the jewelry from him and at the same time, she was annoyed. Beneath those warring emotions ran an undercurrent that saddened her that the gift held no meaning whatsoever. It was simply a beautiful bribe.

"There's something to go with it," he said, smiling at her, and her heart skipped a beat. His bone-melting smiles were irresistible, so her guard came up again because she knew she was treading on dangerous ground. In icy clarity, she realized that with this Ransome her heart was more at risk than it had been with his younger brother.

Matt withdrew another small box and handed it to her. If his motive hadn't been so underhanded, she would have been dazzled. As it was, she gazed at him solemnly, telling herself she could still refuse his offer. Cinderella for a day. She could turn her back on this and survive. But it was beginning to nag at her whether if she did, and lost her big gamble, would she be cheating her baby of a better future?

She opened the box and gasped again. Even when she knew it would hold another beautiful, expensive bauble, she stared at the golden necklace with a diamond pendant that matched her bracelet.

In a smooth movement, he slid onto the seat beside her. "Turn around," he said, taking the necklace from her hand.

When she turned her back, his warm fingers brushed her nape. Reaching behind her head, she held her hair up while he fastened the necklace and then she faced him. He sat close enough that their thighs touched and his blue eyes bore into her, causing her heart to race.

"Thank you. They're both beautiful."

"You're what's beautiful, Olivia," he said softly, brushing a stray tendril of hair away from her ear.

He was only inches away and desire, like heat lightning flashed, holding them locked in the moment. When his gaze lowered to her mouth, she thought he surely could hear her heart pounding. She should move, but it was impossible. She fought the urge to slip her arm around his neck and pull him the last few inches, to draw him close and lose herself in his hot kisses.

"I thought we both agreed we weren't going to do this," she said, as much to herself as to him. She closed her eyes and turned away.

He slipped onto the seat facing her. Even while hot desire still burned in the depths of his blue eyes, the tight clamp of his jaw reflected a tense, angry look in his expression.

"You're right. We'll eat and then get the hell back to the ranch," he said, looking out a window.

"Regrets for bringing me here?"

His head swung around and she braced against the force of his gaze. He shook his head. "Not at all. You should have this. Before long, one way or another, you get a tidy sum of money to buy whatever clothes or car you want. You might as well get some things now."

She bit back her reply when the limo stopped at the front door of a restaurant.

Even though the sun was still above the horizon, tiny lights twinkled in the bushes while large lights shone on tall pines. As she emerged from the limo, Matt took her arm.

They were led through the restaurant past a dance floor where couples already circled to piano music. The waiter seated Matt and Olivia at a table on the patio near a splashing fountain. Brightly colored lanterns were glowing overhead and red roses filled crystal vases on each linen-covered table. In the festive ambience with Matt at her side, Olivia bubbled with excitement.

Their waiter appeared, placing thick black folders with the menu in front of them. Olivia opened hers. She glanced at Matt who was reading his menu and then she looked down at her own. The dishes sounded exotic and the prices astounded her.

"I can't believe we're eating anything as expensive as these dinners," she said.

"The food here is very good," he said. "Do you like lobster?"

She shrugged. "Actually, I've never eaten lobster so I have no idea whether I'd like it or not."

"I suggest you try it and then you'll know."

"The daredevil Ransomes who will always try the unknown," she said quietly, thinking about Matt and Jeff.

"Life is exciting."

"Maybe from your perspective. From mine, life is survival."

"It doesn't have to be from now on," he said smoothly waving his hand to include their surroundings and she was aware again of the clash of wills between them. "My offer will open all the doors for you," he added.

"Marriage wouldn't be real and it wouldn't be permanent," she reminded him and they paused when the waiter appeared.

After they had ordered, she gazed across the table at Matt. "The clothes are beautiful, the jewelry breathtaking and my first flight was thrilling. My first limo ride was unforgettable. But you're not going to hold me with the life you're dangling in front of me now," she said softly. Something flickered in the depths of his eyes. Otherwise there was no reaction from him except an arch of his eyebrow.

"Don't lose sight of the fact that if you turn down my offer, you'll be taking all sorts of opportunities away from your baby. Do you want to raise a child in a neighborhood like you grew up in, instead of the Ransome ranch or a house you can afford in a prosperous neighborhood with a suitable school? You've got to think for two. It's not only you," he reminded her quietly, and her anger soared.

"Dammit, I'm taking that into consideration, but I'm not selling short of what I know my baby should have," she said, hurting because Matt was right. Pain was tight in her chest, and she fought back tears that startled her since she rarely ever cried. His accusation had been on target and hurt badly. But she wanted the Ransome heritage locked in for her baby. "You'll commit to a point and then it stops."

"It's a damn generous commitment, I'd say," he retorted.

"I'll do something to stay out of bad neighborhoods. There are some acceptable jobs out there that I can do and I'll find one. I've gotten farther now than all the odds indicated I would."

"That you have. But don't sell the baby short to try to get me to marry you. Jeff wouldn't, and I'm not going to either."

His words stabbed into her, deepening her hurt. "That's your answer?" she asked, wondering if he would abandon her on the spot. She held her breath while fear chilled her.

"No, it's not my answer. I believe you'll walk so I'm still contemplating the future. I'm not deciding something that important without giving it a lot of thought. Now, on that note, try to enjoy the evening."

"Oh, right," she answered, yet his reply rekindled her hope.

"I mean it," he said in a softer voice. "Had we met under other circumstances, we both could probably enjoy the next few hours. Neither of us will take decisive action tonight, so relax."

"That's a tall order," she remarked.

"It's simple." He stood and came around the table to take her hand. "We'll get away from our problems. Let's dance."

"I can't dance," she said.

He shook his head. "You've got two feet and you can move, so you can dance. I'll show you," he said, ignoring her protest and leading her inside to the dance floor. Her heart drummed as she looked at couples moving so easily together.

"I really can't dance. I never did get around to learning and most of my life has been spent studying and working and trying to survive."

"That's going to change," he said, pulling her into his arms. "Just move with me," he said, holding her lightly. Their proximity was volatile, and every nerve in her body quivered with awareness. As his thighs brushed hers, her desire flamed. His hand held hers against his chest.

She stepped lightly on his toe and almost stumbled, but his arm tightened around her and he held her. "Sorry. I told you—" she said.

"Don't worry. You're a feather and it doesn't matter," he said, interrupting her. "I'm holding you so you're not going to fall," he added in a husky voice.

In minutes it became easier to follow his lead. Even so, when the music stopped she stepped back. "End of first lesson. Let's sit the next one out."

"Fine," he said, taking her arm to lead her back to their table.

When they were seated, over glasses of water and tossed green salads, she paused to study him. "You know a lot about me, but I know very little about you. Jeff was a party boy—he seldom mentioned his family or background."

"He probably talked about himself and his wild exploits. My kid brother and I weren't much alike. At least, I've always hoped we weren't because Jeff was damned irresponsible. What do you want to know about me?"

"Start with telling me about your family," she asked, curious about him because whenever she had approached the subject of family with Jeff Ransome, he had talked about himself.

"There's my dad who has heart trouble and isn't in good health, but he still wants to be in charge and that's why I have my own house. The big house is down the road a ways."

"The big house!" she exclaimed. "I can't imagine one much larger than yours."

"Oh, yes. Bigger, fancier. All it needs is a moat around it and we'd have a castle. I'll take you to see it and meet Dad soon."

"So where do the other family members live? Tell me about Nick and Katherine."

"We're all close in age. I'm thirty-two, Nick is thirty-one and Katherine is twenty-eight. Business is Nick's first love. He's CEO of Ransome Energy and under Nick's control the family oil business has tripled in size, gone public and continues to grow. Nick thrives on making deals."

"Is he married?"

"No. Nick isn't the marrying kind. He's almost as wild as Jeff was, but not quite. Nick is reliable—there's the big difference."

"What about your sister?"

"Katherine has a home in Dallas and one here on the ranch. Nick has his own ranch near ours. She's single and she's a graphic artist, but she specializes in murals. At the moment she's painting one for a museum in Chicago. She's quite good."

"So how long were you married?"

To her surprise his eyes clouded over. "Two years. Margo preferred a career to marriage. Her family is wealthy, so she didn't need the money from the career, but she wanted everything else that went with it."

"What does she do now?"

"She's a news anchor in L.A. now. I suppose in the beginning, I could have gone with her if I'd been willing to leave the ranch and leave Texas, but I have my own agenda and didn't like the idea of tagging along wherever her career led her. Her career is first in her life."

"So you still love her?"

"No, I'm over Margo, but that was a bad time when we divorced. It wasn't what I'd planned."

"And what happened to your mother? Is she no longer living?"

"I don't know," he answered with a cold tone. "When we

were little kids, she walked out on us. There was another man and she married him, but it didn't last a year." Matt's brows arched. "You haven't heard any of this before?"

"No," she said. "Jeff really did focus solely on himself. In spite of that, he was charming and entertaining and drew friends like a picnic drawing ants, but then you know about him. So tell me about your mother. You didn't finish."

"My dad raised us. We've had no contact with her which is the way she obviously wanted it."

"That's dreadful. Do you even know where she lives?"

"No," he said, a shuttered look coming to his expression. "None of us want any contact now that we're grown and she certainly hasn't wanted any since she disappeared out of our lives."

"Sorry."

He shrugged. "That's the way I've grown up. I don't think about it any longer."

"So you're the cowboy in the family who loves the ranch."

"Yes. I get away occasionally. I like to ski and to escape from the ranch. Occasionally, I go to the tropics. We own three ranches, this one, one in Wyoming and one along the California coast and we're buying one we've leased in Argentina."

"As in South America?"

"Right. It's the best ranch of all. It's the one I prefer."

"And Jeff helped you here?"

"Jeff worked with me when he wasn't off gallivanting around the world. He couldn't possibly have settled and worked in an office like Nick is doing. You'll meet my family soon."

"And they approve of your offer to me?"

"Sure. Everyone is interested. A new Ransome in the family would be damn good."

"Seems to me, among the three of you, one of you could produce a grandchild."

"There's already a grandchild on the way." His gaze swept over her. "Have you felt all right?"

She nodded. "Fine. Not even any morning sickness."

"You definitely are pregnant."

"That's a statement and not a question, isn't it? I'm sure you checked that one out and you know who my doctor is."

"Sorry about checking up on you, but I had to be certain."

The waiter brought their lobster dinners. After the first bite, she looked up to find him waiting and watching her.

"It's delicious. You want me to like eating lobster. You want me to cultivate a taste for exotic food."

"I don't know that lobster is exotic. Every grocery store carries them, but I'm glad you like it," Matt answered.

"It's another sales pitch," she said, touching her diamond pendant and knowing that he was doing all in his power to get her to accept his offer and forget her proposal.

"Ma'am, I'm a plain ole cowboy," he drawled, and she had to laugh.

He gave her a wicked look. "Olivia, you're doing your own share of bribery with your smile that seduces and befuddles. You want me to succumb and accept your proposal and you're stooping to as much bribery as I am," he said softly.

"My smile seducing and befuddling?" she asked in mock disbelief, for a moment letting go worries and enjoying his company, bubbling inside because he was flirting.

"You know what you're doing," he said, inhaling deeply and she flashed him another merry smile, wishing she could befuddle him enough to get him to agree to what she wanted.

"Yes! So may the best man—or woman—win!" she exclaimed, holding her water glass up in a toast to him.

Eyes twinkling, he touched her glass with his. "You're on. But then this battle is already under way."

"And you're flirting shamelessly," she said. "Besides the gifts and dinner and clothes and the evening out."

"All my weaponry pales beside yours—your face, your body, your smile, that dress, your legs. You have the edge and you know it."

"Whoo!" She fanned herself. "I didn't know you'd noticed," she purred, enjoying flirting with him. "You have armor that protects you totally. You are shielded and immune."

"Forget dinner. Let's dance," he said, coming around the table to take her hand to lead her to the dance floor. After a few minutes he looked down at her. "You've gotten the hang of it. You're very good at this."

She laughed. "Your flattery overwhelms me! Wait until I step on your toe again."

"I mean it. You're doing fine. Don't you like this?" he asked in a silky voice.

She slanted him a look. "You're flirting again."

"So what's wrong with that? No harm done. You're a beautiful woman and a sexy one. Why shouldn't I flirt?"

"Don't expect it to lead you anywhere."

"Where did you think I want to go?" he asked.

She shook her head and laughed again. "Don't tell me you don't want me in your bed."

"I'll tell you one thing I don't want in my life—any emotional complication. Judging by your demands, I don't think you want any in your life."

"I definitely don't. Not with a Ransome, thank you."

"I take it you and I will never have a handshake deal, even if we finally do come to a mutual agreement?"

"I keep my word."

"I'll damn well keep mine," he said. "Stop mixing me up with Jeff."

The next number was a fast one and when she turned to leave, he caught her hand.

"I really can't do this—" she protested.

"You're a quick study. Watch my feet and then follow me," he said, pulling her with him.

She did what he said and soon she was dancing with him. He spun her around, caught her and then returned to the quick steps. She studied his feet for a few more minutes and then looked up to find him watching her intently. Her heartbeat skipped and she drew her breath, tossing her head and feeling her hair swing.

"Perfect," he said softly.

"Not really. I've stepped on you twice."

"Never felt it. Accept my offer, Olivia, and have a better life and an easier one," he urged. "We're a mere technicality away from what you want."

She shook her head. "That isn't quite the same."

He spun her around and yanked her up against him, his arm banding her waist instantly and holding her close while he looked down at her. She felt his hard length pressed against her and she wanted to wrap her arms around his neck and kiss him. At the same time, she looked into his eyes and felt the clash with him over their futures. She knew the light moments were gone and the flirting was over.

He spun her away from him and then the music stopped. Gasping for breath, she let him take her hand and she felt the calluses on his palm that indicated he really did do ranch work.

"Let's go back to the hotel and talk things over," he suggested.

Knowing they might as well get back to business, she nodded. At the door she glanced back over her shoulder. In the past couple of hours, she had had the time of her life, the best she could remember.

She was surprised by her own reaction and wondered if she had really been in love with Jeff at all.

In the limo she was as silent as Matt, aware they were each locked in separate worlds. At the hotel as they reached their adjoining suites, Matt shed his coat and tie and unfastened the collar of his shirt. "Let me come in for a while. I'll order tea or lemonade or whatever you'd like," he suggested.

She nodded and opened her door, moving inside. He followed and tossed his coat on a chair. "What would you like to drink?" he asked.

"Hot cocoa," she said, wondering if she could drink anything. Her nervousness had returned, but she didn't want it to show. All evening she had felt as if what she wanted was slipping through her fingers. She could feel his resistance to her offer. When he said no, was she ready to make her decision and stick by it?

He ordered a pot of hot chocolate and a cold beer. Only one lamp burned in the fancy suite and in the soft light, his appeal heightened. It would have been easier to deal with him if she hadn't had this fiery sexual reaction to him. And why the chemistry she couldn't imagine because they fought for opposing goals. She suspected he truly did not like her at all. Facing him, she knew part of his attraction was his rugged good looks and a sexiness that probably drew most females he encountered.

He moved around the room, turning on soft music, dimming the light, rolling back his cuffs, seductive moves, yet she knew seduction wasn't his goal. He wanted her to agree to his offer. His control was admirable because she guessed it was an effort for him. She suspected he usually got his way.

At a knock on the door, she watched Matt cross the room in long strides to let the bellman wheel in a cart with a silver pot, china cups and two cold beers on ice. Olivia sat on a wingback chair and crossed her legs. In minutes, Matt handed her a cup of steaming chocolate.

"It's too hot to drink right now," she said, placing it on a coffee table and then leaning back.

When he sat nearby and gave her a long look, she drew a deep breath. "I feel like the proverbial bug under a microscope," she said.

"An absolutely stunning butterfly, maybe. A bug—no," he answered quietly, his gaze drifting lazily over her while she couldn't avoid being pleased by his compliment. "Are you ready to discuss the terms of my offer?"

She shrugged. "It's not essential because I really do not intend to accept it. I prefer that you accept my proposal."

"Let's just say, 'What if?' and talk about my offer for a while. All right?"

"I suppose, as long as you don't abandon me here in Houston if we don't come to an agreement. I do want to return to Rincon."

"I promise to get you home and I don't intend to reach a decision tonight. I only want to talk things over. When I first approached you, we were complete strangers."

"And the brief time we've been together has made a difference?" she asked in surprise because it hadn't changed her opinions.

He set the bottle on a table. "We'll live in my house, but what happens if you want to go out with someone or start seeing someone regularly?"

She shook her head. "You're assuming we will go with your offer."

"Let's discuss it."

"It's pointless to, but if it makes you happy, all right," she said. "For now, I don't want any man in my life. Not at all. You're still going on the assumption that I'll accept your offer and we won't marry. Or do you intend the same agreement if we marry?"

His eyes narrowed and her heart began to thump faster at the determined expression on his face. "No. If we marry, I don't want sordid gossip floating around Cedar County about this baby's mother or stepfather."

"So what do you propose? A celibate life?" she asked, unable to imagine that he would agree.

"Hardly. If I agree to your marriage proposal, I want sex."

Heat blazed in her, and she could feel the perspiration break out on her forehead. While her emotions boiled, they stared at each other. "That isn't what I intended."

"That's what it would have to be."

"How often?" she shot back, trying to catch her breath and wondering if she could handle sex with Matt Ransome without falling head over heels in love with him—a love that she was certain he would never return. Could there be great sex and no love with a handsome man who was helping her raise her child? Hardly.

Fear curled in her, thick and as palpable as smoke from a fire. Jeff had broken her trust and trampled her feelings. Could she expect anything better from his older brother?

"Let's say after your pregnancy is over, twice a week and then we can go from there."

"And until my pregnancy is over?"

"I don't see any need to be definite except if I marry you, then I want a wedding night with sex."

She was certain he could hear her heart thudding. His demands were making both propositions, his and hers, real to her.

"You know what you want, don't you?" Agitated, she stood and moved to the floor-to-ceiling window to gaze down below at the lights on a sparkling pool. Was she ready for sex with him? Her body was more than ready. His words had set her ablaze, but sex was a fast track to heartbreak. Remembering his spectacular, sizzling kisses that had stormed her senses and had been the beginning of seduction, she knew he would be a fabulous lover. And that was what worried her because Matt Ransome seemed as hardhearted as they came.

"There's always my offer," he said quietly, standing close behind her. She hadn't heard him get up or move across the room. She turned to face him. He stood only a foot away. He had rolled back his sleeves and unfastened one more button on his shirt. All she could think of was sex with him—a wedding night.

"If I increased the amount of money, would you accept my offer? If I changed the hundred thousand dollars to a hundred and fifty thousand, how's that?"

Again, he shocked her and she stared at him while the amount spun in her thoughts. "If you're that willing to raise what you'll pay me, then marriage must be binding enough that you want to avoid it at all costs," she whispered.

Matt stood waiting quietly, letting her think about the money. He could afford what he had offered and he did not want marriage, yet standing so close to her, gazing into her wide green eyes, his pulse raced and he was hot with desire. She was stunning with her new hairdo and clothes. She had been a looker before, but now she was breathtaking. Men had watched her all evening in a restaurant where people would be far more restrained than the honky-tonk at home.

No matter how enticing she was, he didn't want a permanent entanglement. Even with the increase in his offer, he felt to his soul that she was going to hold out for marriage.

He inhaled deeply, his gaze sweeping over her slender bare shoulders and long, graceful throat, the soft curves that the dress hugged and her tiny waist. Her long legs were spectacular. He already knew that from seeing her in the towel and cutoffs. Could he take her to bed, live under the same roof, share a baby with her and still keep his heart locked away?

He had no doubt that once she got her law degree, she would be gone. He hoped by that time, she would feel that her child was part of the Ransome family. In the meantime he better worry about the present. What would he do if she turned down his offer?

"I've made you a damned handsome offer," he said aloud, half to her and half to himself.

"I know you have. It was generous before you raised the amount. It's the long-term commitment I want."

"I'll never love again," he said. "You better believe me because I do what I say."

"I imagine you do," she replied, looking up at him. "Jeff told me about how your father got lost one time when his small plane crashed in the Rocky Mountains and after the searchers gave up hunting for him, you flew up there, trekked into the mountains on your own and found him and brought him out of there on a stretcher you improvised. Jeff said you do what you say and you don't give up. Actually, he said you're stubborn as a mule."

"As if he wasn't. I knew my dad was there and I wasn't going to leave him. He had broken one leg and he couldn't get out on his own and no one else survived the crash. My dad is a tough old codger."

"I suspect you're rather tough yourself."

"If so, I've had to be sometimes," he replied, fighting an urge to reach out and touch her. In spite of the conflict between them and his anger, he wanted her. Desire was a throbbing, hot flame tormenting him. She was beautiful and he couldn't stop wanting to hold and kiss her.

"And stubborn?"

"I suppose. If it's stubborn of me to avoid falling in love

again, then so be it. I believe you have a streak of that trait yourself," he said, and she smiled at him. "So you still plan to move
on someday?" he asked

"We both know marriage will give the baby more," she said,
ignoring his question.

Every minute with her he had been torn between anger and
attraction and that was still true. They were at an impasse, and
his desire was escalating. He knew he needed to get distance
between them.

"I'll sleep on it," he said. He strode out the door into the hall,
closing her door quietly behind him and going to his room.

Shedding his clothes he moved around his room. Sleep
wasn't going to be part of his night. Would she walk away from
all he offered simply to hold out for marriage?

He absolutely didn't want to marry again. Not even if the
woman was fabulously beautiful and sexy? The question
taunted him because he couldn't extinguish memories of
holding her in his arms, of her scalding kisses, or how stunning
she had looked tonight. How badly he had wanted to peel her
out of that scrap of a dress! Marriage would mean sex with her.
She had already agreed to it.

He groaned, knowing sleep was impossible. He glared at the
door that led to her room. She would give up most of the cash
if he would marry her, but that didn't matter because cash was
no problem for him.

Coming from the background of poverty, she had a far
smaller regard for money than he would have expected.

Feeling hemmed in and wishing they had flown home tonight,
he paced his room and then moved to the window to stare outside.
It was late and traffic had thinned. He wasn't giving up the baby.
Deep down, he still felt that she would disappear if he rejected
her proposal. "Dammit!" he swore, knotting his fists, wishing he
could walk away. She knew she had what he wanted.

By morning, after a shave and shower, he continued to toss
the choices back and forth in his mind. He went around to knock
on her door and stood waiting, wondering how she had slept.

She opened the door and gazed up at him. Dressed in a white suit and red blouse, once again, she looked stunning. Her hair was looped and pinned on one side of her head, giving her a more sophisticated appearance. No amount of fancy clothes or cosmopolitan hairdos could extinguish her sultry, sexy aura and there was no stopping his body's immediate response to the sight of her.

Matt drew a deep breath. "Good morning."

"Good morning," she replied and stepped back. "Won't you come in?"

As he entered the room, he inhaled the seductive scent she wore. He wanted to tangle his fingers in her hair and pull it down. At the same time he wanted to send her packing. Never since childhood had he had to battle someone and lose as he was with her. Even when Margo left him, at the end he had been angry, but ready for her to get out of his life. He couldn't handle Olivia. It was the first time in his life he had been in this position and he didn't like it.

Staring at Olivia, he was tempted to tell her to pack and go if she wouldn't accept his terms, but when he thought about losing the baby, he clamped his jaw closed more tightly.

This morning she was gorgeous and looked as self-confident as if she already had her law degree. How much easier all this would have been if she had been as plain as a guinea hen. "You're ready to fly home?"

"Isn't that what we're doing?"

"I'm not in a rush. I'll take you to breakfast." They faced each other in a tense silence. "Have you come to a decision on my offer?" he asked and held his breath.

"I still want more than money," she replied nonchalantly as if they were discussing what to order for breakfast, and his insides clenched.

"Dammit, I don't think you know what you're doing!" he snapped, trying to hold back his fury and hating to meet her terms.

"Indeed, I do," she replied with the coolness of a card shark. "So do you have an answer for my proposal?"

He jammed his fist into his pocket. In the night he had made his decision what he would do if she turned down his offer.

"How can you reject the fortune I'm extending to you? You're not thinking about your baby."

"Oh, yes, I am. I can decline your offer because I think you want my baby in your family to such an extent that sooner or later, you'll agree to my proposal. If you do, you'll make a greater commitment than what you're now suggesting I take."

"You're damn sure of yourself," he grumbled, thinking he had misjudged her by a country mile when he first saw her. She was smart, self-possessed and quickly shedding any rough edges she had from her poverty-stricken upbringing.

She merely shrugged. "I'm more sure of you," she replied softly.

He shook his head and rubbed the back of his neck. "I have to hand it to you. I usually get my way in deals. I've bought land, horses, cattle, took over a drilling company for my dad, etc., etc. and you're the only one who's held my feet to the fire and given me something I couldn't cope with."

"Do tell," she said blithely, and he wanted to grind his teeth. At the same time, he had to hand it to her for holding out for the big deal.

"At least, it's a relief to know this baby's going to inherit some brains."

"Thank you, I think. Unless you're referring solely to your brother."

"You know I'm not talking about him."

They stared at each other while silence once again filled the passing time. She smiled at him and began to move around the room, placing her bag and a sack together in a chair so her things would be ready to go. Finally, she turned to face him. "Still debating? We can go to breakfast while you think it over."

Knowing she wasn't going to change, he shook his head. There was no need in prolonging the moment of decision because he was the only one vacillating about her proposition.

Her eyebrows arched and she slanted her head. "No? That must mean you've come to a conclusion? What are you going to do? Are you going to marry me?"

Five

Olivia's pulse jumped because the fury that burned in his gaze made her think there was a possibility he would acquiesce and do what she wanted. While she waited, she held her breath and watched the battle in his tense expression. His blue eyes flashed with pinpoints of fire.

The tension ripped at her nerves and finally she blurted, "What's your decision?"

"You win. I'll marry you," he snapped in clipped words.

Joy and relief flooded her. Her baby's future had just been sealed. It held a promise for the best possible chance for a family, a caring father-figure and education for her baby. And herself. She fought the urge to throw her arms around Matt and shout her gratitude. Instead, she merely nodded and tried to bottle her bubbling response.

"I have some stipulations." He ground out the words, and she nodded.

Like a wave pounding into shore and then receding, her relief swept away and was replaced by worry over what she had gotten herself into. What was he going to require of her in exchange? One condition he had already told her was sex with him! And soon.

"Thank you," she said quietly, feeling his anger that was almost tangible enough to spark the air around them.

He inhaled deeply and gave her another long look that burned like a streak of fire. "We'll have to work out the prenup agreement," he said.

She nodded while her heart thudded. She tried to bank her excitement and keep a lid on all her expectations of what she would gain when she married into the Ransome family.

"Let's get breakfast and make plans," he suggested. "We don't have to check out of the hotel until after lunch, so while we're here in the city, if you want to shop for a wedding dress, I'll give you a list of the stores where I have accounts and you can charge it to me, or if you prefer, I'll go along and write a check or give you a card."

"It's bad luck for the groom to see the wedding dress before the wedding."

He gave her a withering look. "I don't think that old superstition applies in this case. Business arrangements have little connection to superstition."

"I prefer to shop by myself," she answered with what she hoped was as cold a voice as his.

He nodded. "I've already made an appointment for a meeting with my attorney at three o'clock this afternoon. Right now, let's go to breakfast and negotiate the details."

She nodded. "Fine. Give me one minute here," she said, going into the bedroom. She returned shortly and smiled at him. "There. I quit my job."

"That's one good thing," he said.

Picking up her purse, she walked beside him, trying to keep quiet and let him talk. His face was still flushed and a muscle still worked in his jaw. His voice was tight and she could only guess the depth of his anger. She suspected that except for his divorce, he had rarely had to give in to something he didn't like.

Breakfast was in a solarium in the hotel. She doubted if Matt appreciated or even noticed their sunny glass-covered surroundings and tall potted palms. He drank coffee, but otherwise barely touched his breakfast.

While Matt sipped his coffee and studied notes, she remained silent.

"The first stipulation I have, is if you have an abortion or a miscarriage, the deal's off on everything. We get divorced immediately and you get nothing."

"That's fine," she agreed quickly and was surprised at quirk of his lips in a crooked smile. "What's there to smile about?" she asked.

"You won the war. Now you'll let me win the battles," he observed dryly.

She flashed a smile at him. "I can be agreeable and yes, you're right. I got what I wanted on the big issue. Now I can be cooperative on other things."

His expression softened and he studied her, his gaze roaming slowly over her features as if he were trying to memorize her looks. "I intend to get what I want, too," he drawled, and a tingle spiraled in her because she knew he was no longer referring to the prenup agreement.

"So what do you want?" she asked with a jump in her pulse.

"Forbidden fruit," he answered in a sexy tone that fanned flames of desire. "Seduction," he said, drawing out the word until it became personal and enticing.

In response, her throat went dry. "You want sex and you feel lust, but there won't be any love between us or even the illusion of it."

"That doesn't mean it won't be great sex," he replied, looking at her with blatant desire in his gaze. "Are you getting cold feet and wanting out of this marriage proposal?"

She sipped her water and prayed she looked cool and collected and that he didn't have a clue what a tempest he stirred in her. "Be warned now—no love on your part will guarantee no love on my part."

"Do you really want to fall in love with me?" he asked, leaning forward and if she hadn't known better, she would have thought that there was a trace of honesty and vulnerability in his voice.

"At this point, no, indeed not! No more than you want right now—or could—fall in love with me." She raised her glass of water. "Here's to great sex, Matthew Ransome. And a marriage made at the bargaining table."

One corner of his mouth quirked, and one dark eyebrow lifted wickedly. "You tempt me," he said, leaning even closer, "to go after your heart that you've sealed away. And I would if I didn't want to keep my own heart protected. Risk your heart and you risk heartbreak."

"So we'll both be locked in to living together and trying to resist falling in love. And you think it'll be an easy task."

"I know myself and know what heartbreak is," he said gruffly. He reached the short distance between then and drew his fingers along her cheek, sending flames of desire to a scalding temperature. "So you're willing to marry me and have sex to get what you want. You're willing to risk your future."

"I'm securing my future. Not risking it," she said, correcting him and failing to keep the breathlessness out of her voice. "The whole point of this is to take care of my baby," she added, unable to look away from his intense gaze that held her now. Her heart pounded and she suspected if there had been no table between them and they hadn't been in public, he would kiss her. And she wanted him to. Unable to resist, she reached up to stroke his cheek just as he had hers. His jaw was clean-shaven and smooth. The moment she touched him, desire enveloped her with the heat of a furnace.

"You're taking risks, too, to get what you want," she whispered. "Your heart may belong to me someday, Matt Ransome." The clash of wills between them was covered with an icing of desire, creating an emotional dessert that held the potential for spicy, red-hot sex. Goaded by his announced intention to resist falling in love when he planned to seduce her, she leaned the last bit of space and placed her lips on his. Before she closed her eyes, she saw the flash of surprise in his.

Then she was lost. His hand went behind her head and her kiss became his kiss. His tongue thrust deeply into her mouth with possessive, demanding strokes that caused her heart to pound. Her body responded fully to him, aching, on fire with wanting him. They were in public, restrained by their surroundings and with an effort she leaned away. Trying to get her breath, she opened her eyes to find him watching her.

"Sex is going to be great," he whispered.

"I'm going to make you open that vault to your heart," she flung back at him, realizing right now that if they had sex, she would want his love that he kept locked and guarded.

"No, you're not," he answered firmly, but she noticed with satisfaction the perspiration that dotted his forehead and his flushed face.

She leaned closer again. "Let's see how long you can resist me, Matt," she challenged, and he inhaled.

"Don't try to work your magic on me."

"I don't have any magic," she rejoined and his eyebrows arched.

"The hell you don't," he said, tracing her jaw with his finger. "No woman should have the effect on men that you do."

"Do I really now?" she asked, surprised that she had any remarkable impact on Matt.

"You know damn well you do! At least this marriage is going to have some real pluses and some challenges."

"And you like a challenge?"

"Of sorts. I'm not happy about being pushed into marriage."

"You're not being pushed. You can say no. You pointed that out to me on your offer."

"Dammit," he said quietly while he glared at her, and she knew even though he had accepted her proposal, he wished he didn't have to marry her. "We might as well get the questions answered and settled."

He sipped his coffee and looked at the notepad he had placed on the table beside his plate. While she ate a delicious bowl of peaches, she watched him scribble notes. The waiter brought golden omelets, but Olivia's appetite had vanished. So had Matt's because he didn't even attempt to eat, merely reading and writing notes and sipping his coffee.

Determined to avoid letting him know what butterflies she had and how uptight she was, she forced herself to take bites of her breakfast and try to get it down.

"It won't go in the prenup, but once we're married, I expect you to stay faithful. I'll do the same."

She nodded. "Our vows will cover that one."

"You said we'd dissolve our marriage after you get your law degree. As far as I'm concerned, this marriage, if we do enter into it, might as well be permanent."

"Permanent! And what do you mean—if we enter into it? I thought we agreed this is what we're doing."

"We did, but a lot of things can happen between now and weeks or months from now."

She wondered what he had in mind and was there something he was going to do to try to get her to back out of the marriage agreement. And permanent was mind-boggling. "I never planned on permanent!"

"If we're getting married, then a lasting marriage is a good business arrangement. I'll get to raise Jeff's baby, and you'll be educated and provided for and have a family for your baby. Neither of us wants an emotional entanglement, yet we'll have sex in our lives. Who knows—by then, we might be in love."

Setting down her fork with her omelet only barely touched, she drew a deep breath, suddenly feeling as if walls were closing in on her. "I can't envision being married to you for the rest of my life."

"You can always file for divorce if you want out. You know that."

"Yes, but I had no intention of going into this with permanency in mind."

"Can't you see where that would be best for your baby?"

She stared at him. Marriage to Matt Ransome. Permanent as in *forever*. Endless with no emotional entanglement, according to him. Impossible to her.

"You can't do forever?" he asked quietly, and she suspected he was pushing this condition to get her to back off from the whole marriage concept, which she had no intention of doing.

"Yes, I can do 'as long as we both shall live'," she answered, stiffening her resolve to see these nuptials through, "if everlasting is what you want." She would deal with that one as time went by.

"I would like to adopt the baby so it's mine and there's none of this stepdad stuff," Matt declared.

Joy bubbled in her over the adoption suggestion that she hadn't dreamed he would make. She nodded. "Great! That's gratifying to hear."

"I think we said the sum I'll settle on you will be one hundred thousand."

"I told you that you can cut it in half if we marry."

He shook his head. "No. We'll leave it at one hundred." His blue eyes got that piercing look that drove into her like knives. He leaned closer over the table. "One hundred thousand is enough money for you to marry, get the Ransome name and then take the money and run. You could disappear."

"I won't do that."

"Damn straight, you won't! I'll find you," he said with steel back in his voice. She had no doubt that he would do exactly as he said, but she had no intention of running out on the deal he was offering. "Part of our bargain is that you don't run out on me. My mother did that to her family. My first wife all but did that with me."

"If I repeat vows, I'll live up to my promises," she said and gazed back at him unflinchingly. He gave her a long, hard look with icy blue eyes, but instead of chilling her, she faced him and noticed his long, thick eyelashes, bedroom eyes. A lock of black hair fell on his forehead. He had thick hair that held a slight wave and a firm jaw that gave him a rugged appearance, yet at the same time, he was handsome with his straight nose and prominent cheekbones.

She wondered if she was sinking herself in a quicksand of heartbreak. How easy it was going to be to fall in love with him! For all his gruffness and reined-in anger, there had been flashes of charm when they had been out on the town last night, as well as a few minutes ago when he was flirting with her. She had vowed she would never again trust a Ransome or get involved with one, yet here she was committing to the closest possible relationship with a Ransome who had his heart locked away.

"I'll draw up a will. I own the ranches with my father, brother and sister and we want them to stay in the family. If something happens to me, my share will go directly to the baby when he or she reaches twenty-one. The money I have will be divided between you and to the baby. Fair enough?"

She nodded. "For a man not in love with me, you're making another generous offer."

As he inhaled deeply, she wondered what was running through his mind because she couldn't possibly guess. Somehow she suspected he was wishing he could have the baby and get rid of her, but then she might be wrong.

He shifted and his knee bumped hers. His eyes narrowed while she felt a tingle from the contact.

"I need to meet your family," she said.

"I know. I'll get them together."

"You're not touching your breakfast," she said quietly.

"I don't have any appetite," he replied, biting off the words abruptly. He fluctuated between flirting with her and then giving way to his suppressed fury over having to acquiesce to her wishes. In the moments when his charm and appeal surfaced, she found him irresistible.

She suspected after marriage he would accept their bargain and then she would have his charm and sex appeal to deal with daily, a possibility that gave her a tingly anticipation and at the same time, sent warnings of heartbreak pounding in her mind.

Where Matt's brother had been an engaging fun-filled boy,

Matt was a devastating man with charm and sex appeal that overwhelmed her.

"I don't think we'll have an issue about the baby's education since you fought so hard to get one," Matt said, scribbling more notes while she nodded.

"I'll still open an account for you with the one hundred thousand in it. That is your money. I'll pay the ranch expenses, etc. and open a joint account for us."

"You continue to surprise me," she said, again amazed by his magnanimity when she knew he was unhappy with her.

"We might as well work together. We're binding our lives together forever," he added and she wondered about her future with him. "Hopefully," he continued, "we'll stop fighting each other."

She laughed. "I wouldn't count on that one," she exclaimed, leaning closer. "You intend to seduce me. You want my body." She placed her hand over his on the table. "If you do, I'll warn you now—I'll seduce you because I'll want your heart."

"I thought you were going to try to avoid another heartbreak."

She shook her head. "We're on a different course since I made that declaration. We're marrying, and you're making it permanent. If that's the case, and we'll be intimate, then I want more than lust and a purely physical relationship for the rest of my life. I want love."

"Once again, you want more," he repeated, smiling at her. "Where have I heard that before? Only this time, you won't have the leverage you did about marriage." He turned his hand to take hers and rub his thumb across her knuckles, stirring tingles. "You're flirting with me, Olivia."

"So I am. Don't deny that you like it."

"Of course, I like for you to flirt and to kiss. As you said, we're stuck with each other now, so we should make—" he paused and desire heated his gaze "— love, as well as the best of it," he finished in a velvety drawl that held its own caress. "I'll have to say that you're damn cooperative now that you've got what you want."

"I try," she said, bestowing a smile.

He laughed and straightened up, releasing her hand. "I'll get you a wedding ring. We need to make some decisions about the wedding first. How about a small wedding?"

She tingled at the prospect and wondered if she could go through with this loveless marriage of convenience—even with Prince Charming, which Matt had been on occasion. "That's fine," she said, but her words were breathless and her head spun. Marriage—and then she would be in Matt's bed. Sex with Matt Ransome! Again she thought about sex with him—over and over she thought of it. Her palms felt sweaty, and she watched him writing in his notebook. If he was disturbed or gave the notion of sex with her any of his attention, he was hiding it well.

"I'll pay the wedding bills, of course," he continued. " If you don't have a particular church, we can be married at the ranch. The only people I want to invite will be our cowboys and my family."

Trying to get back to thinking about what she was doing instead of sex with Matt, she mulled over his suggestions and shook her head. "You're so concerned about my baby—which will soon be our baby. Maybe you should think about inviting a lot of your friends, too. Otherwise, I'm not too likely to be accepted by some people because of my background and where I've worked," she said, and he nodded.

"You're right. Good decision."

"Why do I get the feeling that from the first, you've expected the worst from me?" she asked.

"Maybe I misjudged you. You constantly surprise me. But it's for the good, so that should be all right," he admitted. "We'll have the whole deal, a big wedding and reception."

"Why not a small, private wedding and then the big reception?"

He shook his head. "I'd say the big wedding because I want people to accept you as much as any other member of my family and there will be a reluctance by some locals for the reasons you said and because you were close to my brother who had a reputation for being the wild man of the county."

"I'm three months pregnant."

"Won't matter. You don't look it anyway. I'll hire someone to work with you to plan this wedding."

"If we have a big wedding, it will take time to plan."

"No. I'll hire a wedding planner who can get everything ready. I'll call family and close friends. Word will get around before the invitations. You get your wedding dress right away," he said, starting a new list, writing while he talked. She wondered exactly how much wealth the Ransome family had because Matt didn't seem daunted by anything except her proposal.

She had butterflies dancing a ballet in her stomach at the thought of a big wedding with all his family and friends present. "Matt, I don't have any family and only a few friends."

"Doesn't matter. Most of the county will come to the wedding and lots of people from other counties and from Fort Worth. Matter of fact, guests will come from everywhere because my brother and sister get around. By the way, you have carte blanche on this."

"You already trust my judgment?" she asked.

His gaze drifted down over her as far as he could see with the table blocking his view and then back up in a leisurely, thorough study that curled her toes and made her forget business. "You have good taste. You look like a professional woman this morning—like the lawyer you will be someday. Last night you looked fabulous. I think I can trust you with the wedding decisions. I'll help with the wedding at the ranch because we've had so many catered parties there. I already have a battery of people who can handle all aspects of the reception. We should open an account for you today."

She nodded, growing more dazed with each of his quick decisions. It all seemed like a dream, magical, impossible, yet the man beside her was real enough. And the most fabulous, awesome aspect of all—her baby would officially be a Ransome. Matt would help raise him or her.

What was impossible to put out of mind and ran in an undercurrent of thought all the time they talked was the far more immediate prospect of sex with Matt—getting naked with each other. The thought stirred a burning low in her middle. And would there ever be more than lust and a baby between them?

He pulled out a small black book, flipped it open and scribbled in it, turning to hold it out to her. "How's this date for our wedding?"

Stunned, she stared at the black circle he had drawn and then she looked up at him.

Six

"I couldn't possibly!" she exclaimed while she stared at the date circled—next Saturday. "This is Monday! This week—not even a full week to get ready for the biggest event in my life, a complete life change, an enormous wedding with your relatives and friends. Impossible!" she exclaimed, trying to ignore a feeling of panic that surged while she reminded herself this had been her idea and she was getting what she desired.

Part of her wanted to ask for a year to get ready. The other part would like the wedding as soon as possible, to lock her into the Ransome family before something happened that changed Matt's mind or made the wedding impossible. Next weekend—it sounded the same as tomorrow.

His blue gaze settled on her. "You're quiet. Getting cold feet?"

"Never," she replied emphatically. "I want this with all my heart."

While they looked solemnly at each other, she knew they each had different goals for their futures. And they each would fight for what he or she wanted. She knew that, too.

He glanced at his watch. "We should select invitations today. I'll get a list of guests and get someone at the Ransome office to address the invitations and get them out at once."

"Matt, we can't do this in a few days. Give me another week at least."

"All right. The date will be the following Saturday," he said with assurance in his tone. "Let's go. I have calls to make, and you can shop for your wedding dress. We can meet back at the hotel for a late lunch around one. When we fly home, we'll go to Fort Worth and open a bank account for you. How's that?" As he talked, he fished his billfold out of his pocket, withdrew a credit card and flipped it over on the table so it landed in front of her. "Buy whatever you want," he said casually and she stared at him. "Or if you don't find what you want, we can go to Fort Worth to shop. Or Dallas."

"I'll find something," she said, quietly. "Thank you."

"And you're surprised again, aren't you? You must think I'm a green-headed ogre."

"No. I'm simply amazed you're so generous when you're angry with me. And I didn't know your family had such wealth," she said.

He gave her a dubious look. "C'mon. That's common knowledge in the county. It runs back to the fortune my great-granddaddy made on cattle and land."

She shook her head. "Your brother flashed money, but no more than a lot of other cowboys and until he left for the mountain trek, he didn't do anything that made him look particularly prosperous except play poker. He never took me home with him, so yesterday was the first time I've ever seen the Ransome ranch."

Matt shrugged and gave her a rueful smile. "You get your way on the future for both of us, so why should I stay angry or try to keep things from you when you'll be my wife next week?"

Wife next week. She was glad she was sitting down because her head spun at the thought of becoming Mrs. Matt Ransome so soon.

"We pick up and go on from here," Matt continued. "I don't want revenge because you and I are going to be a unit. From here on, it would be like fighting myself."

"And you're not?" she asked softly, unable to resist flirting with him now that their future together was sealed.

"Not what? Fighting myself?"

She smiled at him. "You don't want to be attracted to me. It aggravates you that you want to kiss me."

"Maybe so," he said, leaning close enough again to start her heart pounding. "Sooner or later, we'll work things out. I just usually manage to get my way and this is one time that I haven't."

"Maybe I can keep you from regretting your decision," she said in a throaty voice. "If we both try, Matt, we can have a good marriage."

He wrapped his fingers around her hand again. "I'd like that," he said and leaned close. "Just remember, I warned you that I'm not going to love again. And remember the old saying: 'All's fair in love and war'. You've had all the forewarning that I need to give."

"And so have you," she said with a smile. With her free hand she stroked his nape lightly.

His eyes darkened, and she knew she was taunting a tiger that could bound to life and devour her heart so easily. "I'm beginning to look forward to this, Olivia," he said softly. "And I look forward to our wedding night and having you in my arms." While he talked he reached up to wind locks of her hair in his fingers, tugging so lightly, yet making her aware of his touch.

Her pulse raced and her mouth was dry. "Twelve days from now, I hope we know each other better."

"You've learned a lot about me already and I know some about you. And I'll answer any question you want."

She tilted her head to think a moment. She was curious about him and had a multitude of questions, but she tried to choose the most urgent. "Are you still in love with your ex?" she asked, and a shake of his head gave her pleasure.

"Not even in the tiniest fraction. If she wanted to come back tomorrow, I wouldn't want her to, but she won't want to. She's in love with her job. And then with herself. When we were married, I made a threesome." He waited expectantly.

"When you were growing up, did you and your siblings get along with your father?"

"Well enough," he answered easily. "Our father can be a dictator and a lot of people are cowed when they deal with him, but we've grown up with him and his fiery temper and determination."

"Are any of you a lot like him?"

"I hope not," Matt replied. "You can ask me more later. Right now, let's go," he said, gathering his papers and standing, coming around to hold her chair.

As soon as they separated, Olivia began shopping for a wedding dress.

When she slipped the cool silk of the first one over her head, her heart thudded at the sight of her image.

The white dress was a dream. Tendrils of her hair had tumbled free and fell around her face and she had to admit that she thought she looked pretty, but it was the wedding dress and what it symbolized that held her speechless. She was dressing for her wedding for a marriage of convenience that she was going to contract to for the rest of her life. With a man who was angry with her, accustomed to getting his own way, and determined to avoid ever falling in love with her.

Would her baby's future be worth what she was willing to sacrifice, Olivia asked herself, because she suspected that no matter what she did or felt, Matt Ransome wasn't going to fall in love with her. The image in the mirror that stared back at her was a wide-eyed woman in a wedding dress about to marry—in less than two weeks—in a loveless marriage.

If she had good sense, she would guard her heart, too, she thought, turning to look over her shoulder at the dress. She guessed it would take a long, long time for Matt to forgive her for pushing him into this marriage of convenience.

Would his family accept her?

She suspected that would be one of the least of her problems.

She removed the dress and tried one that was white satin with a full skirt and cathedral train. Every moment of the past two days had held a dreamlike quality, but seeing herself in wedding dresses was surreal. She was going to marry a week from Saturday!

She ignored the pang that tore at her heart. This wasn't what she had planned for herself, but then nothing had gone as planned since she had met the first Ransome.

An hour later, she found the dress she wanted and knew she needed to look no further. She turned first one way and then another as she studied her reflection while she smoothed the skirt to a white sleeveless silk with a low-cut V-neck and straight, plain lines with a removable train. The simple elegance and flattering style made it the dress she wanted.

In another hour her head spun with her purchases of a veil, shoes and wisps of lacy undergarments. She stopped in a bookstore to select some books on pregnancy and baby care. When she glanced at her watch, she realized she would have to race to get back in time to meet Matt at the hotel.

When she arrived, he was in the lobby, seated with papers spread in his lap. At any moment she expected him to back out of their bargain. Soon she would be Mrs. Matthew Ransome. When the time came, would he go through with the ceremony?

As she approached him, his gaze assessed her, and she tucked a wayward tendril of hair behind her ear while her pulse jumped.

Watching her cross the lobby, he waited until she was only yards from him. He gathered his things and stood.

"Sorry I'm late," she said breathlessly. "I have boxes in the cab."

"You should have called," he said, walking beside her to go back outside to retrieve her packages.

"I don't own a cell phone," she replied, amused that he would automatically assume everyone he knew had a phone. He gave her a quick glance and reached into his pocket to hand her a phone.

"Take mine for now. I can get another easily." Matt took her arm and she was aware of his body warmth as she walked close beside him. She could detect a hint of barberry aftershave that was as tangible as his hostility. Yet he had accepted her terms. Marriage to a Ransome. One minute she wanted to kick her heels in the air and shout for joy. The next minute she wanted to pack and run.

He opened the cab door to retrieve her packages and move them to the waiting limo. Looking at an enormous box tied in white ribbon, he remarked: "I see you found a wedding dress."

"Yes, I did and it's bad luck for you to see me in it before the wedding."

Matt gave her a mocking grin. "You're worrying about me seeing your wedding dress?"

"All right, maybe that's foolish."

Their limo driver transferred her packages. "You should have let us pick up your wedding dress," Matt said.

"They placed it in the cab for me and I knew you would get it out," she said.

When she climbed into the waiting limo, Matt slid into the seat facing her. "Did I tell you this morning that you look beautiful?"

"Thank you," she replied.

"Perhaps we can make this arrangement halfway work."

"I hope it works completely," she admitted, wishing momentarily that she really could have it all—including a marriage with love. "It'll be a fraudulent marriage in some ways," she said quietly.

"This morning over breakfast I think we settled that we can make a marriage of convenience more palatable," he said.

"Maybe with time," she replied.

"While you shopped, I got a wedding planner," he said, handing her a slip of paper with a name, address and phone number scrawled on it. "You have an appointment in Fort Worth tomorrow afternoon at one."

"That was quick."

"For parties at the ranch we have a regular caterer and a band, so I've hired them for the wedding."

Olivia stared at him and wondered if she was getting entangled with a dynamo who would try to take charge of every aspect of her life.

"You're giving me a look," he said. "Do you disapprove?" he asked, startling her by guessing what was running through her mind.

She shook her head. "No, I'm a little overwhelmed."

"I doubt that," he remarked drily. "I've contacted our family minister and we'll have the reception at the ranch."

"You've done it all," she said. "Except buy my wedding dress."

He shook his head. "Not quite. We both need to get attendants. The wedding planner will have a florist and a photographer and you can arrange with her for the wedding cake. The big deal is telling my family. I suspect it may be a bombshell. I'll warn you right now, my dad may be difficult. Katherine might be, too, but it's dad who intimidates people. If you want, I'll see to it that you never see him without me until after the wedding."

Amused, she gazed at Matt. "You think he'll scare me out of this? If so, I'm surprised you didn't send him to talk to me before you accepted my proposal."

Matt smiled. "I don't think my dad will frighten you away, but you may not want to deal with him alone. I think you're a match for him which is saying something, believe me. Not many people can hold their own with him, but I bet you will. And if Katherine gives you a hard time, I'll deal with her, too. As soon as we get back to the ranch, I'll call them."

"Fine," Olivia said, wondering what kind of confrontations she would have with his family.

"When you become my wife, you won't need that law degree," he remarked.

Startled, she gazed back at him in silence while she thought about it. "I want to get an education. With the arrangement we have, I don't know what I'll need in the future."

"You can think about it," he said. "I moved my afternoon appointment with my attorney to tomorrow morning at ten. We'll both meet with him to go over the prenuptial agreement."

"That's fine, too."

Soon they boarded the private jet. When the plane taxied down the runway and soared into the air, she looked down at the city spread below and knew she would never forget the past night or today. Her gaze lifted to the expanse of blue sky that stretched endlessly in her view.

Once they were airborne, she heard him writing and turned away from the window to see him poring over his notes. Until he wanted her to talk to him about something specific, she was going to look out the window. It was her second flight in an airplane and she was still dazzled by it.

"Olivia," he said and a tingle spiraled in her.

"Yes?" she replied, giving him her attention.

"I want you to agree now that you'll stay with me. I don't want you to get your law degree and then take your child, divorce me and move away. Of course, if you're going, I can't hold you, but I want in the prenup that you won't get anything of mine if you leave. And I'll want joint custody."

"That's fair enough. I'm sure I can find legal work in this area. I want to practice law when I pass my bar exams."

"I can keep a child with me a lot of the time when I'm on the ranch."

"You don't know the first thing about taking care of a child, do you?" she asked.

"Nope, but I can learn. What kind of experience have you had in child care?" he asked, and her cheeks flushed hotly.

"Maybe none, but this morning I bought some baby books that I intend to study. Also, I think that child care is more likely to come to me innately than to you," she replied with a haughty air.

"We won't argue that one. Time will tell," he replied, drawing circles on her knee with his finger. She was aware of his touch and the warmth of his gaze and she wanted to lean toward him, to brush his lips with hers.

"Later this month I'm in a rodeo in Jet. The event is bronc riding. Will you come watch me ride?"

She nodded. "You always say your brother was the wild one. Seems to me bronc riding is on the wild side."

"Not so much. We do that on the ranch just for the fun of it."

She turned back to look out the window while she thought about the man she was marrying and what an enigma he was.

The rest of the day was dizzying. As soon as they landed in Fort Worth, Matt whisked her to a bank downtown and they were ushered into a thickly carpeted office where she watched with perspiring palms while Matt signed papers and deposited twenty thousand dollars into an account for her and put the remaining amount of money into a savings account. She was stunned to walk out of the bank a wealthy woman with an account and money to spend any way she so desired.

"Matt," she said, placing her hand on his arm while he stopped and looked down at her.

"Thank you. I never dreamed I would have money, not until I'd maybe practiced law forever. When I become a lawyer and pass the bar, I'll repay you," she said.

"Don't be ridiculous. We're getting married. I don't like having my money and your money. It's ours. If you contribute, fine. If you keep what you make for yourself, fine. If I marry you—even in a paper marriage, Olivia, then I'll share my bank account with you unless you go hog wild with it."

Amazed that he would allow her full access to his fortune, she could only stare in speechless wonder.

"Okay?" he asked when she didn't respond.

"Of course it's all right," she replied hastily. "I am constantly taken aback by your generosity. I can't even imagine someone sharing like you're willing to do."

He stopped and turned to her and she felt as if she were drowning in pools of blue. "Olivia, next week you'll become my wife. That's the way you wanted it. We'll have a bargain that I intend to live by for the rest of my life."

For the first time, she realized how permanent the approaching marriage of convenience would be. "Suppose you fall in love with someone?" she asked, wondering again what she had gotten herself into—for that matter, gotten both of them into.

"I won't."

"You can't know that! No one knows what will happen when love is involved."

"I'm not going to fall in love with anyone. My money will be your money as long as you handle it reasonably well. You don't have to repay the money I put in the bank account for you today."

"I'm absolutely stunned over what you're doing," she admitted, knowing every small detail of this moment would be etched in her memory forever. Wind blew locks of his black hair and his blue eyes were intent on her. A faint smile hovered, deepening creases in his cheeks. Besides Matt, the passing crowd, the sound of cars, the heat of sunshine—she would remember this event that in her wildest imaginings she had never dreamed would happen.

"Are you all right?" he asked.

"Yes. Just bowled over by your magnanimity."

"I'm just doing what I want to do. You can show me your gratitude tonight," he drawled in a husky, sensual voice that strummed across her nerves and set them quivering. As the same time, his eyes twinkled, so she didn't know whether he was teasing, goading her into something, or really meant it.

"I'll think about it," she said, giving him a saucy toss of her head.

He chuckled softly as she turned to walk to his car.

Finally they returned to the ranch and when they entered the house, Matt tossed his keys on the kitchen counter. "I'll call my brother and sister tonight. In the meantime, I'll grill steaks and we can make more plans. Where do you want this dress? You can keep it in another bedroom so it won't crowd you."

In minutes they had all her new purchases in another bedroom, and she had agreed as soon as she changed clothing, she would join him for a swim.

While she hurried to get ready for the swim, his words

echoed in her head: "You can show me your gratitude to-night." Had he meant that? Was he going to want sex before the agreed time because of the money he had given her? Or had he been teasing? If sincere, then he was in for a surprise because sex for her new bank account was not part of any bargain they had struck.

Before she left for the pool, she took a long look at herself in the mirror. She had bought a new black two-piece swimsuit that was cut low on her belly, high on her hips. She studied the changes in her body, aware that her breasts were fuller. Her stomach was still flat and she ran her hand over it, thinking about her baby. A girl or a boy? She was beginning to want to know and not wait another six months to be surprised. She wondered whether or not Matt would want to know.

Satisfied with her looks, she twisted her hair and pulled it up in a ponytail. She grabbed her cover-up, a big towel and flip-flops before going to the sparkling blue pool. Matt already had fired up the grill and the smoking mesquite smell was tantalizing.

As she walked across the patio where cool air was piped near the house, Matt bobbed up in the pool, and raked his hair away from his face, giving him a harsher, more rugged look. Water glistened on his broad shoulders, and her pulse began what was becoming a familiar racing.

He watched her approach and her heart thudded at the slow, thorough perusal he gave her from head to toe. His gaze lingered on her breasts and on her stomach, drifting down over her legs and she was on fire by the time she neared the pool.

He pulled himself up out of the water with a splash, sending cold drops sprinkling her. Her pulse was already racing, but now her heart thudded as she looked at him clad in only a scrap of black suit. His skin was tan, glistening with water, muscled, lean and hard. He was studying her, but no more than she was eyeing him and she couldn't resist staring. While her heart pounded, she marveled again that soon—tonight possibly—she would be in bed with him.

"If I hadn't seen the doctor's report myself, I'd never believe you're pregnant. You don't show at all," he said in a husky voice, walking closer.

With each step he took, her drumming pulse beat faster. She barely knew what he said as she looked up at him. They wore only bits of clothing and she knew he was as aware of her bare body as she was of his. And she wanted his lean hard body against hers. She could feel heat creep into her cheeks over the way she had been ogling him.

"How in heaven's name did you get my doctor's report? That's private," she asked, annoyed. "I may call my doctor about that."

He shrugged. "Who knows what my P.I. did, but he had the report. Your doctor may not have known someone looked at your record." Matt jerked his head toward the pool. "Come in. The water's great."

He made a running dive into the pool, swimming away from her. She followed, sliding into the cool water to swim. At the end of the pool she clung to the edge, shook water away from her face and found him beside her.

"You're beautiful, Olivia," he said in a husky voice. "I think we may have made a damn fine bargain."

"Those aren't exactly the magic words that every woman wants to hear two weeks before her wedding."

His eyebrows arched. "We're going into this like any business deal. You surely didn't expect hearts and flowers."

"No. That's not one of my stipulations. Last night was great because it was memorable to go out and not be reminded at every turn that what we have between us is a contract."

"You do want more," he observed and moved closer. "This is one thing we have between us that isn't in the contract."

Seven

He slipped his arm around her waist and drew her up against him. The moment she touched the length of his warm, hard body and legs, her stomach did flip-flops. When her hands went to his shoulders, desire exploded in her.

Sliding her arm around his neck, she looked at his lips and then glanced up to see him looking at her mouth with hungry longing. When he bent his head and covered her mouth with his, her heart pounded. Time and thought stopped. She lost all sense of where she was or what she had been doing. She was in his arms and he was kissing her senseless and she was coming apart at the seams over his kisses.

His arm tightened and his arousal was hard against her belly. Desire shook her. His free hand moved over her shoulders and throat and then slid down her front. While he continued to kiss her into oblivion, he held her away a fraction. His hand unfastened the halter top she wore and peeled it down, baring her breasts.

"Matt!" she exclaimed, ready to protest, remembering that she was going to show some restraint with this Ransome, but his fingers stroked her nipple and her protests melted. Warm and wet, his hand cupped her breast while his thumb circled her nipple slowly, making her moan softly and thrust her hips against him and want him with a need that shocked her. She twisted slightly to give herself access to him, sliding her fingers over his thick rod.

He growled deep in his throat as he kissed her. Then he leaned down to take her nipple in his mouth, teasing with his tongue, stroking and circling her taut bud.

"Matt!" she gasped again, unable to tell him to stop, knowing she was already breaking her promises to herself. How would she resist him twelve more days when she was letting him do what he wanted now? Did she want to wait until after they were married?

Desire surged, and she trembled as she kissed him and responded to his hands playing over her, first on her bare breasts and then sliding down over her belly. His hand slipped into the bottom half of her swimsuit and he found her soft folds, stroking her so lightly, yet setting off more blazing fireworks.

"You're so damn responsive to me," he whispered.

She tangled her legs with his and ran her hands over him, feeling his muscled body and firm bottom.

In minutes she knew there would be no stopping for either one of them. She pushed lightly against his chest and twisted away. He caught her arm to hold her.

"Matt, don't go so fast. I'll be in your bed soon enough."

Desire blazed in his eyes. An intense yearning that made her heart pound as violently as his passionate kisses had. He placed his hands on her waist and lifted her up out of the water and she placed her hands on his shoulders.

His gaze drifted over her bare breasts, slipping lower. "You're beautiful!" he gasped and her heart jumped.

How could she possibly keep from falling head over heels in love with him? He was devilishly handsome, rugged, sexy. He could be charming and she had the feeling that he really hadn't turned his charm and lovemaking on full force as far as she was concerned.

She didn't doubt that he meant what he said about keeping his heart locked away. Could she really scale the walls of that fortress?

She looked into his blue eyes and all she could see was desire so blatant it made her nipples tingle again. The heat low in her body intensified.

With his gaze locked with hers, he lowered her slowly, holding her closer and letting her slick, wet body slide against his. His hard shaft slipped between her legs and she gasped with desire that swept her with the force of a tidal wave. Closing her eyes and clinging to him, she knew she had to stop him right now and she needed to get out of his arms and get some distance between them.

She wasn't going to fall into his arms and into his bed and succumb to his seduction on the third night she had known him.

With an effort, as he leaned forward and his lips brushed hers, she splashed away from him and scrambled to pull her suit back into place. She looked over at him and saw him treading water while he watched her with a faint smile.

"Scared of me? Or scared about your own reactions?" He waved his hand. "Come on back. I can show restraint."

"Sure you can," she teased lightly. "Catch me," she said and turned to swim away as swiftly as possible.

He caught her easily and hauled her into his arms, laughing with her, but as their legs tangled and he held her close, their laughter vanished, replaced swiftly by need.

With pounding pulse, Olivia wriggled away. "Not yet, Matt," she said, wondering how long she could wait.

He swam past her and climbed out, grabbing up a towel and tying it around his middle. He shook water away from his face as he slicked back his hair. "I'll get out the steaks and pour glasses of iced tea."

Getting out of the pool, she watched him cross the patio and her mouth went dry as her gaze drifted over his broad, powerful shoulders and muscled back that tapered to his tiny waist and tight bottom. Abruptly, he halted and glanced at her, catching her staring at his body. He turned around to stroll back to her and each step closer he came to her, the more loudly her pulse pounded until she was certain he could hear it.

He placed his hand under her chin. "Go ahead and look. What you see will be yours to play with whenever you want," he said in a velvety voice. He stroked her cheek and let his fingers lightly slip lower, caressing her throat and pushing open the cover-up to fondle her breasts. "And what I see will be mine to play with and make love to, I hope."

"I believe that was part of our bargain," she whispered, unable to get any firmness in her voice. Was she already falling in love with him even before her wedding?

How disastrous would this bargain be to her heart? A bargain with a demon of her own creation. She could have taken the money, lived with him and waited to see if they fell in love instead of this headlong rush into marriage to get a commitment for her baby.

It was done now and she wasn't backing out, but she should take care and guard her heart more than she had so far. Two days ago she wouldn't have dreamed she would be at risk of heartbreak.

He looked over at her. "Penny for your thoughts."

"I was just mulling over what odd turns life takes and a week ago this time, my life and prospects for the future were entirely different."

"Regrets?"

"Absolutely not. Never! I couldn't possibly regret the changes. What about you? This morning you were filled with anger."

"We'll see what the future brings. Let's sit down and go over some more stipulations."

Amused, she smiled. "You're trying to think of everything. That's impossible."

"Maybe, but I want some requests. I'm in no hurry, but I want a DNA test to determine that there is no question that my brother was the father."

"That's fine," she said. "He was, so test away." She sat at a wrought-iron table on a cushioned iron chair, crossed her legs, catching Matt staring at her bare legs.

He pulled on a T-shirt over his swim trunks and then dropped the towel. The T-shirt hid his swimsuit and it was easy to imagine him without it and she hoped he had no inkling that she was doing so.

"Do I get a say in the baby's name?" he asked, pulling his chair close and stroking her knee, starting more fiery tingles.

She thought about that one. "I think we should both approve the selected name," she said breathlessly, only half aware of what she was replying to him.

He moved closer and placed his hands on her shoulders. "We've already learned that we can get along and the sex promises to be great. We both have mutual goals about the baby. But make no mistake, Olivia. I'll never fall in love again," he reminded her.

Annoyance flashed in her at his stubborn refusal to even give love a chance and then she thought how far she had already come with him. She slanted her head and smiled at him. "At the moment, I'm not after your heart. But when and if I decide I am, you may find that you don't have such a fortress as you thought."

"You've been warned."

"So have you," she said, and interest danced in his eyes. His gaze lowered to her mouth. She started to turn away, but he caught her, kissing her and lifting her onto his lap. Their legs were warm and bare and her pulse thundered while passion possessed her.

Matt leaned down to kiss her possessively. While his tongue stoked a fire in her, his arm banded her waist tightly. His other hand slipped down over her back and across her bottom, heating her desire.

Wrapping her arms around his neck, she twisted to press against him while she kissed him in return, pouring all her need into the kiss. She could feel his arousal hard against her and his free hand roamed over her while his hungry kisses demolished her intentions to resist him.

With desperation, she broke free, gasping for breath and satisfied to see his breathing was as ragged as hers as they both gazed at each other.

"Olivia, I don't think my life will ever be the same again."

"You can bet the ranch on that one," she whispered, standing and wanting to stay in his arms, wanting him to love her the rest of the night. She swept past him. "I'll dress for dinner," she called over her shoulder without looking back at him.

She hurried to her room for a cold shower, lecturing herself about resistance and caution and self-control and gaining his respect. She dressed in a denim sundress, sandals and caught her hair up in a ponytail. There was no way to stop unruly tendrils from escaping and curling around her face. She leaned forward to glare at her reflection.

"Get some control," she whispered. "You're mush when he kisses you." She didn't want to even think about his devastating kisses. But if he was leaping over barriers around her heart, she suspected she might be building bridges over his. "Just you try to resist falling in love with me, Matt Ransome," she declared.

She straightened up. "Yeah, right," she said, reminding herself that the man had iron willpower, and he could probably keep his heart locked away for a lifetime if he chose to. She thought about Jeff's story about Matt rescuing their father when all the professional rescuers had pulled out of the area. Jeff said Matt refused to give up, but he wouldn't let Jeff or Katherine search with him and Nick had a sprained ankle. She was dealing with a man who had a will of iron and would make all kinds of sacrifices to get what he wanted.

Would her heart break over this hard, tough cowboy? And beneath the wealth and sophistication, she suspected there was a cowboy who was a lot of country.

She squared her shoulders and smoothed her skirt. She was willing to take some risks. At this point she had the world to gain—and only a broken heart to lose, she reminded herself.

With a toss of her head she left to join him for dinner.

By the time she strolled onto the patio, he was grilling

steaks. A plume of gray smoke spiraled above the cooker and tantalizing smells made her mouth water, but it was the tall, handsome cook who took her breath and made her pulse jump.

He had dressed in slacks, western boots and a knit shirt, but how easily she could remember the body and muscles beneath those neat clothes. He glanced at her and then turned to give her his full attention, watching her walk toward him.

Tingling and growing hot, she sauntered up to him, stopping only inches from him. "Like what you see?" she asked in a sultry voice.

A faint smile quirked his mouth. "My anticipation about our wedding night is growing," he replied and her pulse jumped another notch.

"It'll be even better than you imagine," she said.

"You're flirting again, Olivia." He ran his finger just above the top of her sundress, drawing a line on her bare skin that made her draw her breath. "But why do I think you have an ulterior motive? I think you want me to fall in love with you so you can steal my heart away and twist me around your little finger." His fingers trailed upward to her nape where he caressed her lightly. "Am I right? Or will you admit the truth?"

"I'll answer honestly," she replied, wanting to kiss him instead of chat with him. "I hadn't thought about twisting you around my little finger and I don't really believe that I possibly can. Maybe I'm just trying to protect my heart so if I do fall in love with you, I won't be rejected."

He propped his foot on an iron chair and placed his arm on his thigh as he leaned closer. She was hemmed in by him and by his leg on one side of her, the cooker on the other and the chair behind her. His blue eyes pierced her as if he were searching for answers in her gaze. "So you're not getting cold feet yet over our deal?"

"Of course not," she said, acutely aware of his proximity and his leg touching her hip lightly. "We need to talk about the wedding. How many attendants will I need to have because you'll have groomsmen."

"Back to business? I'd rather talk about making love."

"We better take care of business if you want this wedding next week."

He smiled at her and traced the curve of her ear. "All right. How many attendants do you want?" he asked in a husky voice and she suspected he was giving little thought to the approaching nuptials.

"You're not thinking about our wedding," she said.

"I'm thinking about making passionate love to you on our wedding night," he answered in a husky voice and leaned down to brush her lips with his.

Her heart thudded, but she fought her impulse to kiss him and stepped back. "Matt, we have to make decisions about the wedding. How many groomsmen? I have three friends here, but I can well imagine that you will have a lot more close friends, plus your brother. I'll be happy to ask your sister to be an attendant."

His heated gaze kept her pulse racing. "All right. We'll discuss the wedding—for now. I've been trying to get in touch with my family to let them know. While you dressed, I tried to call Nick and Katherine. I've left messages for both of them."

"Are they here in Texas?"

"No. I called their cells. Katherine is in Chicago, and Nick is on a rig in the Gulf. I talked to my dad and of course, he wants to meet you. We're having him join us for breakfast in the morning. How's that?"

"Fine," she said, wondering if his entire family would disapprove of her and try to talk Matt out of the marriage. For an instant a surge of panic threatened, but then she reminded herself that Matt had agreed to marry her and he said he would keep his word.

Matt caressed her nape and she stopped thinking about his family. "Three attendants will be fine. If you want her, ask Katherine," he said. "I can't predict what she'll do or say."

"I hope they don't hate me."

"If they do, do you want to call off the marriage?"

"No, I don't."

He tugged on a curling lock of her hair. "Dad will be the most difficult to deal with. He's not the same since Jeff's death. Jeff was his baby and his favorite which is why he let Jeff do just what he damn well pleased."

"If I have a boy, I don't mind if you want to name him after your brother."

Matt traced his finger around the curve of her ear. "That might be a real fine thing. It would mean a lot to the whole family. 'Course you may be having a girl."

"When the time comes, I'll find out what my baby is going to be. When I have an ultrasound, you can even go with me if you want."

His eyes narrowed. "I'd like to go with you," he replied. "I'd really like it," he repeated as if surprised by his own feelings. "Something else—as soon as we marry, I wish you'd refer to this baby as 'our' baby, even though I'm not the blood father. For all intents and purposes, I will be this baby's father."

"That's wonderful!" she exclaimed, delighted with his suggestion. "Our baby," she repeated, the words thrilling her. Then she focused on him again. "You're standing close," she said quietly.

"It bothers you?"

"You know you disturb me," she replied.

"If the steaks weren't going to burn, I'd do more to disturb you right now," he said in a husky voice that was its own caress. He walked to the grill to take the steaks off and set them on the table.

Hunger pangs increased her anticipation, but when she sat down at the table across from Matt, she lost interest in food. Talking to him and making wedding plans took precedence over eating. As they chatted, she couldn't believe her good fortune.

Over dinner Matt charmed her with stories about the ranch and his brothers and sister, yet all the time he talked about them, Olivia couldn't stop wondering how much they would accept her and the approaching marriage.

She barely touched her steak and noticed that Matt didn't either. They talked about a myriad of subjects and she wondered if his life had been lonely before, but then she pushed that notion aside as ridiculous. Matt could do as he pleased and she suspected he kept busy all the time. Looking into his thickly lashed blue eyes, she couldn't imagine, in spite of what he had said, that there weren't women around often. His handsome looks and virility took her breath. If only—she dismissed that thought immediately. She was getting more than she ever dreamed possible. She had to stop looking for love.

The sun set and lights came on automatically in posts scattered around the patio. The pool sparkled with light and she was dazzled by her surroundings, but far more by Matt. He reached across the table to take her hand in his. His fingers were warm and strong. At the intense look in his eyes, her pulse speeded.

He reached into his pocket with his other hand. "I bought a ring for you today while I was waiting," he said and placed a small black velvet box in her hand.

Surprised, she opened it and her heart missed beats when she looked at the dazzling diamond that sparkled against the dark velvet. "Matt!" she gasped, stunned by his gift. She looked up at him. "It's fantastic!"

"You like it?" he asked.

"Of course, I love it!" she said. "It's magnificent! I can't believe you would do this! We barely know each other. I'm astounded—" She realized she was babbling, but she was caught off guard and never had expected any such ring.

"Olivia," he said, cutting short her words and leaning closer to slip his hand beneath her chin. "For this baby's sake, we're entering into a marriage of convenience, but as far as I'm concerned, I think it would be best for our baby if all our friends think we're in love. You'll get a hell of a lot more respect that way, and men will leave you alone. Unless you let them know they don't have to leave you alone."

"Don't worry about that one," she said. "We've already agreed to be faithful to each other."

"At this point that's merely lip service."

"Not for me," she said, solemnly, her excitement diminishing. He took the ring from her and slipped it onto her finger.

"It's a perfect fit," she said, wiggling her fingers slightly and watching the huge diamond sparkle. "This has to be the biggest diamond I've ever seen in my life."

"Good. It's eight carats and that should be big enough to keep guys away and earn you respect from the women."

She looked at the glittering diamond and then at him. He was being generous beyond her wildest dreams. She pushed back her chair and walked around the table and something flickered in the depths of his eyes. As she approached him, he scooted his chair and she sat on his lap and wrapped her arms around his neck. "Thank you," she said and leaned down to kiss him.

His arms enveloped her and he shifted her closer, kissing her in return until she forgot all about the dazzling ring and was lost in Matt's kisses.

His hands brushed her bare shoulders and nape, sliding down to twist free her buttons. He pulled down the front of her sundress to cup her breasts in his hands. When his thumbs drew circles on her nipples, she moaned with pleasure, a sound that was muffled as his tongue plunged deeply into her mouth.

Then his hand was beneath her full skirt, pushing it high while his fingers caressed the inside of her thigh. He turned her on his lap so he could slide his fingers into her lacy panties.

"Matt!" she gasped.

Shifting her over him so she was astride him, he cupped both her breasts and lowered his head to her breasts, to kiss first one and then the other. He drew his tongue in slow circles around her nipple while his thumb continued to circle her other nipple.

Bombarded by sensations and desire, she clung to his shoulders and then let her hand slide down to his hard shaft. With a pounding pulse, she unbuckled his belt and unfastened his trousers, trying to free him from the restraints of clothing. She wanted him totally, yet she clung to her resolution to wait until their wedding night to give herself fully. She refused to fall into his arms and his bed so quickly even though every caress and kiss was fueling the bonfire that consumed her.

Lost to his lovemaking, she moved her hips while trying to fight through the fog of need back to caution and patience.

Catching his wrist, she held his hand. "You're going too fast again." She swung her leg over him and straightened her clothing, trying to pull the top of her dress back in place.

His blue eyes had darkened with passion and the heated look in them made her heart pound. When he fastened his clothes, she returned to her chair and studied her new ring. "I've never dreamed of owning jewelry like this."

She looked at him and her heart missed a beat because the desire in his expression shocked her.

"I want you, Olivia. I want you in my arms in my bed and I want all that passion you have bottled up turned loose."

"You have to wait only a few more days," she reminded him, wondering if either one of them could resist that long. Already, they weren't able to keep their hands to themselves and when they started kissing, they almost lost all restraint.

"Let's clean this up—"

"Nope," he said, standing and taking her hand and crossing the patio to a cushioned glider. "Later. Let's sit and talk."

Olivia moved to a chair close to the glider and received a mocking smile from Matt. She looked at the ring again. "This is absolutely fabulous. Thank you so very much."

He nodded. "Wedding dress, ring, minister, wedding planner, caterer, band and lawyers. We need to get in touch with my family and get our attendants lined up. Your attendants will need to get dresses. As soon as we go to the courthouse tomorrow and take care of the legal stuff with the county, I think we'll have everything else in order."

"I can't believe you're getting all this done this quickly," she said, knowing she could always expect him to try to take charge and go at a gallop to get what he wanted.

"We have parties out here and some of the arrangements aren't that different," he said.

Butterflies flitted in her stomach at the thought of talking to the rest of the Ransome clan.

Matt took her hand, lacing her fingers in his. He raised her hand to brush her knuckles with kisses, his warm breath a caress that made her want back in his lap. As she talked about classes she could take in the fall, Matt scooted his chair against hers. Finally, she stood. "I insist we clean. Mrs. Marley won't be here tonight or tomorrow."

He waved his hand. "Sit and talk. I'll clean. It'll give me something to do because I'm not going to sleep."

She wrinkled her nose at him. "I'm not going to ask why you won't sleep," she said as she sat again.

"You know exactly why," he replied in a low voice. He reached over to lift her into his lap.

She wound her arms around his neck and smiled at him. "I think we did this a short time ago."

"I can't remember," he said, looking at her mouth.

She inhaled and pulled his head down as she placed her mouth on his to kiss him, knowing every kiss made her want more. "Matt," she whispered, kissing him between words, "you're making it harder to wait—"

"Darlin', you're definitely the one making it harder," he drawled in a sexy innuendo that she barely heard over her pounding pulse. Matt's arm tightened around her and his tongue went deep. He kissed her long and thoroughly before she made him stop again. Standing, she moved away. "I'll see you at breakfast."

He gazed at her with a smoldering intensity and she hurried away, knowing a few more seconds and she would have been right back in his arms.

That night she was restless, worrying about Matt's father and how his family would accept her after learning she had talked Matt into a loveless marriage of convenience.

Tuesday morning at breakfast, she could feel the tension in spite of Matt being charming and his father chatting easily. Duke Ransome was a large, powerful-looking man with shoulders as broad as Matt's and a deeply tanned complexion.

Dressed in western shirt, jeans and boots, he still was a handsome man. He had brilliant blue eyes and a scar across his temple that was a testament to his rugged ranch life. He could be as charming as Matt, but his smiles ended before ever reaching his cold blue eyes that continually bored into her.

It was no surprise to her when breakfast was over and they moved to the family room to have Duke look at his son and announce, "Matt, I'd like to talk to Olivia for a few minutes, just the two of us."

"I'd be happy to talk to you, Mr. Ransome," Olivia said, trying to sound collected. She had dressed with care and was thankful in her shopping yesterday that she had bought a new, tailored navy suit and matching silk blouse. Ignoring her churning stomach, she hoped she looked poised with her hair looped and pinned behind her head.

"Dad, I think anything you have to say might be well said with all three of us together," Matt suggested.

"Nope. I want to talk to Olivia. I'm not going to bite her head off," Duke said and smiled at her, but it was a smile that chilled her and she wondered what he intended to say.

"I'm staying to hear whatever you have to say," Matt said in a voice that was as firm and direct as his father's and she knew at this point the decision was between the two males so she remained silent.

"Very well," Duke said and nodded, motioning to her. "Please sit down."

She sat in a leather wingback chair and Matt perched on the arm of the chair beside her.

The moment Duke Ransome turned his steely gaze on her, she braced for trouble. "You know we're all interested in your baby and want the baby in this family because it's a Ransome," he began.

"Yes, sir. Matt has made that clear and that's why we're marrying," she replied, aware that Matt remained silent. She wondered if he and his father had planned this talk together and hoped to get her to back out of the pending marriage.

"Which, of course, was your idea. I know my son doesn't want to wed again, for convenience or any other reason."

Olivia merely smiled and waited. Duke Ransome moved to the window and looked out at the sprawling ranch land. "We've fought for this land and protected it and I've struggled to keep my family together. I miss Jeff. This baby is his child and is a part of him."

"Yes, sir," she said, wondering if he intended to try to stir her sympathy. Questions swirled through her thoughts and curiosity about Matt plagued her. Why was he silent? Was he hoping his father would drive her away?

Duke Ransome turned to face her and his gaze chilled her. "There's no love between you and Matt because a week ago you didn't know each other and I know you haven't fallen in love in the short time you've known each other. Matt is not in love, I'm sure."

"No, sir. We haven't fallen in love," she admitted. "But we think we have a good arrangement."

"Maybe I can give you a better one than Matt can. I don't want you messing up my son's life. And that's what you'll do." She started to speak, but he raised his hand.

"Hear me out. Give us Jeff's baby. You're a beautiful woman and you'll fall in love again. You can have a lot more babies. Give us Jeff's baby and I'll deposit in your account a half of a million dollars to let us have the baby and you get out of Matt's life permanently. You can add this amount to what Matt has offered and you can keep the ring he's given you. In total, my proposition, plus Matt's offer and his ring will be well over half a million."

Eight

Stunned, Olivia stared at him. After surprise shook her, her mind began to function. "Thank you for your generous offer, but my answer is no."

Duke's eyes narrowed. "Did you hear how much I'm willing to give you? You can't turn down that much money."

"I can and I have," she said quietly. Matt's arm curved around her shoulders and he gave her a squeeze.

"You haven't even thought it over," Duke said, scowling at her.

"I've kept quiet, Dad, to hear your offer, as well as to hear Olivia's response," Matt said in a firm voice. "Just now Olivia refused you. That's what I wanted to hear. She's honest and true and up-front about all of this. You and Jeff have both underestimated her and misjudged her just as I did before I met her. In my judgement of her, I was off a country mile and you're even more mistaken about her. Just as Jeff was. Jeff couldn't see beyond a desirable woman."

"Dammit! Neither can you!" Duke snapped, his voice rising. "Don't be taken in again. You married a woman who couldn't wait to dump you. You don't know anything about women, Matt. Stop interfering here."

"I'm not interfering. Olivia just refused your offer."

"You don't think this baby needs its mother?" Olivia asked, her anger increasing by the second.

"No," Duke replied, his attention shifting back to her. "We'll make up for that. My children grew up without their mother and they turned out fine."

"Perhaps they did," Olivia replied. "From what I knew, as charming as he was, Jeff cared about no one but himself." She glanced at Matt who gazed back with an unfathomable expression. "Matt is cynical and talks about his sister and brother being wild," she continued and turned to face Duke again. "All of your children might have benefited from a mother's influence."

"By any standards my family is a fine one," Duke said, and his face flushed a deeper red. His anger was palpable. Olivia regretted she was the cause of it, but she wasn't intimidated by Duke Ransome and she had no intention of giving up her baby for any amount.

"I didn't say they weren't a fine family, Mr. Ransome. I just think a mother might have had an additional positive impact on them. My baby is going to have its mother. Your family puts too high a priority on material things." She tried to bank her own smoldering anger and think clearly because she was making monumental decisions about her future and her baby's and she didn't want to make the wrong choice in an emotional, knee-jerk reaction.

"I think that's a bit difficult to accept coming from a person with your background and your demands on my son. You can't tell me money means nothing to you," Duke said, gruffly.

Matt stood and placed his hand on her shoulder. "That's enough, Dad. A week from Saturday Olivia and I intend to marry. We're working out a good arrangement that will give our baby a father and a mother and a family and financial support."

"Financial support! Like hell!" Duke's fiery gaze bored into Olivia. The room snapped with tension, yet she felt insulated, certain about what she wanted and reassured by Matt's stand against his father.

"The tramp will take you for as much as she can get!" Duke exclaimed, still staring at Olivia.

"Tramp?" Matt put his hands on his hips, clenching his fists and taking a step toward his father. "I don't think so," he said in a chilling tone that made Olivia draw a deep breath. "She turned down your offer of half a million dollars—that's no tramp after money, Dad, and you better face the truth. She's going to be the mother of your first grandchild. You owe Olivia an apology."

"Matt, please," Olivia said, standing and placing her hand on Matt's arm. "I don't want to cause a rift between father and son."

"Like hell you don't," Duke snapped. "In your lifetime you'll never have such wealth as I'm offering. If you marry my son, you won't be able to touch the Ransome money. Matt will see to that."

"I'm not after cash. There are other things in life that are important."

"I think you're after the Ransome fortune and I'll do everything in my power to keep you from getting a dime of it."

Olivia could feel the waves of anger emanating from Duke. His fists were clenched, and his face flushed a deeper red.

"Dad, you're on dangerous ground—" Matt said, stopping when she squeezed his arm.

"Wait, Matt," she said and turned to his father. "Mr. Ransome, it's not the Ransome money that I'm after. I'd like my baby to be part of this family that he or she belongs to by blood, although after the past few minutes, I am having second thoughts about that. From what I know so far, Matt is an honorable man. I would like a father for my child. My baby is a Ransome, therefore, I would like my baby to have the benefits of being a Ransome, but not at a price that will compromise his or her life in any manner. Frankly, you, sir, make me want to walk out of the door and never look back. Your son, on the other hand, has accepted my proposition for a marriage of con-

venience that will give *our* baby opportunities beyond anything
I can ever offer."

"Damn straight, you little—"

"Dad!" Matt snapped in a tough, determined voice as he
stepped forward with clenched fists. "Apologize to the woman
I intend to marry and to the woman who is the mother of your
grandson! You damn well apologize or you'll never know this
child. I'll cut you off right here and now."

"Matt. Don't!" Olivia stepped in front of Matt, placing
herself between the two angry men. "Stop this! Don't let me
tear apart your family," she urged. Her heart pounded and she
was cold with worry, wondering if Matt even saw her or knew
she was in front of him. His blue eyes flashed with fire and his
chest heaved.

"Get out of the way, Olivia," Matt said without taking his
gaze from his father.

"No! I won't let you two destroy this family," she said.

"If you reject my offer, you'll regret it all your life," Duke
said, lowering his clenched fists and turning to look at her.

"I'll never regret turning down your offer," she declared.

Duke glared at Olivia. "You're a cool customer, Miss Brennan.
If you're holding out for a better offer, you won't get it."

"Sir, I've already gotten it," she said softly, and his jaw
tightened. Matt stepped beside her and placed his arm around
her shoulders.

"Dad, you apologize to my fiancée or don't come back to
my house or to our wedding."

Olivia bit back a protest at Matt's threat because she wanted
a united front with him, but his ultimatum to his father hurt. She
never intended to rip apart a family.

"You have my apologies," Duke snarled in a tone that clearly
indicated his insincerity. "There—you have your damned apology." He looked at his son's arm draped across her shoulders.
"I hope both of you know what you're doing," Duke said.

"I think we do," Matt answered.

"You give long and thorough consideration to my offer,"

Duke said to her. "It would set you up for life. You know that you can have other babies and you know that we would provide a truly good life for Jeff's child. There's not a shred of love between you and Matt."

Olivia and Duke held each other's gaze for a tense moment. "I won't forget your offer. It was interesting to meet you, Mr. Ransome."

"You watch your step, missy. I'll do everything I can to talk my son out of marrying you."

"I think your son probably makes his own decisions."

Duke nodded. Striding from the room, he slammed the door behind him.

She let out her breath and turned to face Matt. "I hate that you and your dad had such a fight."

Shaking his head, Matt raised his eyebrows. "Dad didn't tell me what he was going to do, although I should have guessed. I'm sure he thought he'd made you an offer that you couldn't possibly refuse."

"Half a million to give you my baby and get out of your life."

"I'm a little amazed you could so quickly and easily turn down that amount."

"None of you get it—you can't hang a dollar sign on a child. I'm not giving up my baby."

"I didn't ask you to with my offer. I wanted you to let us share Jeff's child's life."

"I won't give up my baby for any amount. I didn't have to think about my answer."

Matt studied her and put his hand on her shoulder. "Dad doesn't know you at all and he thinks everyone can be bought."

She ran her hand across her brow and Matt placed his finger beneath her jaw and tilted her face up. "Upset?" he asked.

"This past hour hasn't been the easiest time in my life," she said, trying to lighten the moment, but she felt weak in the knees and anger still smoldered inside. As much as she wanted to ignore Duke Ransome and forget his hurtful words, his "tramp" accusation rang in her ears and it hurt.

SARA ORWIG 113

"I doubt if your father will attend our wedding."

"Oh, yes, he will. I know my dad. Did it ever occur to you that you could be getting into a union that you'll hate?" Matt asked in a quiet voice while reaching out to trace his fingers along her cheek. "Soon I'll be the legal father and have as much say as you in our child's life."

Our child. The words slipped across her raw nerves, reminding her of all the changes that were soon coming because of her decisions. "I'm willing to take the chance. I think we'll work out an arrangement we can both accept," she said, hoping she sounded cool and Matt didn't have an inkling of the butterflies she had over the thought of her future shared with him and his family.

"If I ever worry about you holding your own with my family or anyone else, remind me to forget my concern," Matt said. "I've seen some tough men that couldn't cope with my dad. You won that round with the old man," Matt added. "There are a lot of people who've had tough times, and they would've taken the money and never looked back. I think Dad lumped you in with that group." Matt studied her, his gaze going slowly over her features and making her pulse drum.

"Thanks for standing up for me."

Matt shrugged. "You gave him your answer. He should've accepted it and his remarks were way out of line, but he's accustomed to getting his way and doing whatever he has to do to succeed. I misjudged you a hell of a lot more than a country mile," Matt admitted. He leaned forward to brush a light kiss on her forehead before glancing at his watch. "We need to go to town to the attorney's office. If we don't leave now, we'll be late."

"I'll get my purse," she said, gratified by Matt's remarks and his support.

"Meet you at the back door," he said and left the room with her, going the opposite direction when they reached the hall. Halfway down the hall, she glanced over her shoulder to find him still standing where she had left him. His hand was on his hip as he watched her. When she looked at him, he turned and disappeared into his office.

Matt went to his desk to get a briefcase that held papers and notes he had made for the prenuptial agreement. Half his thoughts were on the coming appointment. The other half were on Olivia and his father. He was astounded his dad offered her so much money, but by now, he wasn't surprised that Olivia had turned him down. She wanted marriage and all the commitment that went with it, even if it was going to be a business arrangement. A lot of people would have wilted with his dad and given in to him, but also, by now, Matt knew Olivia better. She was a strong woman who would not be intimidated by his dad or outsmarted by him. If the situation hadn't involved such high stakes, it would have been amusing because few people refused his dad.

Matt knew he would hear from his father soon to try to persuade him to back out of the approaching marriage.

Matt had no intention of backing out. Each day it looked like a better proposition. They would have an acceptable arrangement for living together; the baby would be his to share—he would become the adoptive father; and he would have sex on a regular basis with Olivia. If the marriage arrangement worked, he could imagine they might drift into loving each other, but in the meantime, he never wanted to go through heartbreak again.

Later, in the car as he drove into town, Olivia shifted on the seat to face Matt. "I guess your father is never going to accept me," she remarked.

"Once you present Dad with his first grandchild, he'll accept you so quickly that you'll be astounded. Believe me, I know my dad. He's wanted a grandchild, dreamed about one, harassed my sister to get married, harassed me when I was married to give him an heir. No, he's going to love your baby and you won't be able to believe that he offered you a fortune to get out of our lives. You'll see a transformation that will astound you and Dad will act as if nothing disagreeable ever happened."

"I'll believe it when it happens," she said unable to imagine Duke Ransome changing so drastically.

"My dad probably expected you to jump at the chance for a fortune because you didn't grow up in comfort."

"Comfort!" She laughed. "There were nights I slept on buses because it was safer and more peaceful than going home. My parents drank and—" she stopped abruptly. "You know all about my background. When I was in high school, I'd just ride the bus at night so I could study. I always felt education was my passport out of that life and it has been."

"That's what I mean. Dad and I misjudged you badly."

"Now I only have to face your brother and your sister."

"I still haven't been able to get in touch with Nick or with Katherine, but I'll keep leaving messages for them."

"They'll probably try to talk you out of this wedding, too. They know we're not in love." She looked at her ring and wriggled her hand. "I think the rest of the world will be fooled about it."

"Don't be surprised if you get some other kind of offer from my dad. He doesn't give up easily."

"I'm not worried."

"No, I suppose you're not," Matt said. "You continually surprise me."

"For one reason or another, most men I've met have misjudged me," she admitted. "That first night you certainly did, and I'll bet your P.I.'s report about me was not at all what you expected."

"You're right. But then, maybe I've surprised you. Because of my brother you prejudged me." Matt smiled at her. "I haven't had a chance to tell you, but you look like you're worth a million today. You look gorgeous," he said. She could see the warmth in his gaze and his compliment pleased her, taking away some of the tension of the past hour.

"You sweet-talkin' devil. You'll turn my head," she teased, momentarily forgetting the raw differences between them, giving him a mocking, coy look that made him grin.

"The more I know you the less I dread this wedding."

"Just watch out, Matthew Ransome," she said, leaning across the front seat. "First thing you know, you'll be in love with your wife," she said and laughed, straightening up and scooting back into her place.

"You would do that when I'm driving," he remarked,

shooting her a quick glance before his attention returned to the road. "Remind me later what you said. And I'll tell you again. I'm not falling in love with anyone, Olivia. All women are romantics and sometimes they pay a high price for it."

"Is that right?" she asked with such sweetness in her voice that he scowled.

"Time will tell, but you're in for more heartache if you're going into this contract thinking I'm going to fall in love soon."

"I think you've made it quite clear that you're a man with no heart. But no matter how much you declare that, Matt, you have a heart and you've loved before, so there's a chance you'll love again. You won't if you shut yourself off from everyone, and I hope you don't do that with this baby because if you want to be a real dad, then you'll have to open your heart."

"That's different and I will."

"Then just take care that if you get your heart functioning again, it doesn't do things you hoped to avoid."

"I'll take care," he answered with a cynical tone. "You better worry about protecting yourself."

"You sound defensive. You're getting angry and you're a tad beyond the speed limit. I think I see a flashing light behind us," she said, looking in an outside mirror.

"Oh, hell!" Matt snapped, and she had to bite back laughter because she knew she had goaded Matt into losing some of that iron control he had. She remained silent while he pulled off the road. When the patrolman approached the car, Matt greeted him.

"Hey, Ebby," Matt said easily, extending his hand and shaking the patrolman's hand when he leaned down to look into the open window. "Ebby, meet Olivia Brennan, my fiancée."

"You're getting married?" the man asked without hiding the surprise in his voice.

"Sure am. You'll get an invitation to the party soon," Matt said.

"Howdy, Olivia," the trooper said in a friendly voice, and she smiled at him.

"Look, my attention was on my fiancée and I just forgot

what I was doing," Matt explained easily. "You know how it is. You and Tamara just got married what—five months ago?"

"That's right. Five months and one week. Look, just slow down a little and try to think about your driving. I'll give you a warning this time, Matt."

"Thanks. I sure will go slower."

"Nice to meet you," Ebby said to Olivia and she smiled in return and twisted in the seat to watch him walk to his car and soon pull around them.

"You got yourself out of that one," she said as Matt drove onto the highway.

"Remind me to put his name on our invitation list."

"You're driving quite sedately now," she observed. "All we both have to do is to hang on to our cool through the prenup agreement."

She received a crooked grin. "You think I can't do that, don't you?"

"I don't have any idea. I don't even know what you want in the agreement."

"You know most of what I want because I've discussed it with you before."

In a downtown building in Fort Worth, she entered the large reception area and in minutes a short, blond man with lively brown eyes approached them and shook hands in greeting with Matt who then introduced her.

"Vic Waterman, this is Olivia. Olivia, meet Vic."

"Glad to meet you," he said, shaking Olivia's hand while he smiled at her. "Both of you come with me and we'll find a quiet place to work."

In a paneled conference room they sat at an oval table and Vic Waterman produced papers and a legal pad. While Matt opened his briefcase to take out his papers, she waited quietly.

For the next two hours they went over prenuptial details. At one point Matt said that he wanted it clearly stipulated that if she divorced him, she forfeited any claims on the Ransome money for herself. When he gazed directly at her, she nodded.

"I find that quite acceptable," she answered easily, watching Vic Waterman write in his tablet.

Finally they worked out an agreement that was to Matt's satisfaction as well as her own. Trying to contain her excitement, she was thrilled with the contract that would protect her in many ways and provide for her baby.

The closer she came to becoming Matt's wife, the more anticipation she experienced. She wanted the ceremony over and done, her baby's future secured. As she glanced at the handsome man she would soon marry, her pulse jumped. How much was she looking forward to the wedding for her baby and how much for herself?

How many times would she remind herself that she was going into a loveless marriage? Was she a hopeless romantic as Matt had declared? Was she dreaming of the impossible, of a man who would fall in love with her? Did she want him to and would she fall in love with him? She knew she was already doing exactly what she had promised herself she would never do—stop guarding against heartbreak.

If something happened tomorrow and she had to walk away from all this, Matt included, she could do it without hurt, she was certain. Would she feel that way in a month? She glanced at him again. Leaning back in his chair, he had pushed his coat open. His self-confidence was obvious. He was handsome, sexy and exciting. If he dreaded their approaching nuptials, he didn't show it. And she hoped she didn't show her nervousness either.

She looked into Matt's blue eyes. It was impossible to tell what he was thinking—whether he hated her for this or if he expected a satisfactory arrangement. She bent her head to skim over all the points they had thoroughly discussed.

Finally they were finished and told Vic goodbye. In the lobby of the building Matt turned her to face him. "You have the appointment this afternoon with the wedding planner. Let's grab a bite to eat and then we can separate and meet later to go home."

She nodded and walked two blocks with him to a small restaurant that was busy with a lunch crowd.

"Feel like celebrating? You're getting what you wanted," he said as soon as they were alone in their booth.

"Yes, I'll celebrate. And you protected yourself with the agreement we just signed, so you should be satisfied."

"Actually," he said, glancing at his watch, "what is going to satisfy me is my wedding night with you," he said in a husky tone that changed the conversation. He reached across the brown wooden table to draw his fingers along her arm and her heartbeat quickened while she drew a deep breath.

"See, that's what I like. You have an instant response to me." He leaned closer over the table and lowered his voice. "You're the sexiest woman I've ever known."

"I seriously doubt that one," she said, suspecting he flirted without giving it thought.

"I'm telling the truth. You're sexy and you respond to the slightest attention. Right now, you've got me aroused and hopefully, I've done the same to you."

"Please remember that we're out in public."

"Believe me, I wouldn't be sitting over here and you over there if I didn't remember that we're not alone. But that doesn't mean I can't touch you," he added. He slipped his hand beneath the table and caressed her knee, sliding higher along her thigh.

"Matt!" she exclaimed while heat rose from deep within her and her desire intensified.

"No one can see me. We're in a booth and it's dark beneath the table. No one cares what we're doing. I want you alone with me, in my arms, but more than that, I want the night to come when you're in my bed and I can make love to you."

"You stop now," she said breathlessly, knowing she had the firmness of jelly in her tone. His light strokes along her leg were stirring feelings she didn't want to have now, making her want to be in his arms and making her want to reach for him in return.

A waiter approached their table. With a mocking smile, Matt straightened and leaned back in his seat. She ordered a salad and listened to Matt order a burger. Then they made plans for the afternoon, but now she was more aware of Matt than their conversation and it was difficult to concentrate or talk about appointments and buying clothes and running errands.

After lunch they separated, agreeing to meet in three hours. She walked a short distance and turned to look in a store window, but instead of seeing the display, she watched Matt striding away. He was tall enough to spot easily in the crowd of people on the street. Wind caught locks of his black hair and he had a long purposeful stride. Saturday night and seduction. She still wondered if she would last until a week from Saturday without trying to seduce him or letting him entice her into sex.

Fishing in her purse, she produced a list of purchases to make. Her engagement ring flashed with brilliant fire in the afternoon sunshine and she was still amazed that Matt would give her such an expensive gift.

She met with the wedding planner, and then shopped and finally went back eagerly to meet Matt, hurrying because she didn't want to be late and keep him waiting.

That afternoon at the ranch Matt shut himself in his office to take care of business. In her room, she changed to cutoffs while she remembered the last few minutes with Matt. "When your wedding night comes, Matthew Ransome, I'm going to make love to you like you've never been loved before," she said, knowing she wanted this marriage to work. She crossed the room to the mirror to study her image. "Are you falling in love with your fiancé?" she asked her image softly. She looked down at the brilliant diamond he had given her. He was being too good to her, too appealing and his kisses too devastating. Was he seducing her into an illusion of love?

"You knew you were in for heartbreak," she told her image.

She pursed her lips, remembering kissing him. "But so is he," she said softly. "The men in this family have had their way far too long."

She patted her stomach. "I've turned down two fortunes for you, so I hope you know how much I already love you," she said quietly. "*Our* baby." Matt wanted her to refer to the baby as *our* baby. Excitement fluttered in her. She was going to have a family for her baby. A father, grandfather, aunt and uncle.

Staying out of Matt's way, she explored the house. In the library, she roamed around the room, looking at leather-bound volumes that were shelved along with dog-eared children's books that must have been Matt's and his siblings'. She opened cabinets to find more books and then she found a closet with shelves of scrapbooks. She looked at dates on labels on the spines of the books and pulled out some from years earlier to look at pictures of Matt as a child. She enjoyed pictures of his brothers and sister, studying them and able to pick out Jeff's cocky grin and Matt's usually solemn expression.

After she had worked her way through a stack she noticed a large gray metal box on a shelf. The box was dusty and looked as if it hadn't been touched in years. When she tried to open it, she couldn't.

Curious, she lifted it down carefully because it was heavy. She placed it on the floor and sat beside it to try to get it open, but was unable to until she discovered a tiny brass key taped to the bottom of the box. Puzzled, she stared at the key a moment. Why would someone bother to lock a box and then tape the key where anyone could find it?

She pulled the key away and unlocked the box. A chill ran down her spine and she had a premonition of disaster. Shaking away the feeling as ridiculous, she opened the box.

Nine

Four books were in the metal box. Lifting them out, she saw that they were baby books. She glanced through them and found Matt's, then replaced the others in the box. The pages in Matt's book crackled when she opened it and she wondered how long since anyone had looked inside. She read his birth announcement and then she saw baby pictures. Turning a page, Olivia looked at a stunning young woman with black hair and movie-star looks.

This was her baby's grandmother. Olivia turned the pages slowly, looking at Matt's baby pictures and his parents. Duke was thinner, younger and undeniably handsome. Matt's mother was beautiful and Olivia stared at her picture. How could this woman walk out on her four children?

Matt insisted his father would love his new grandchild. What about Matt's mother? Was there a chance she'd had regrets through the years? Would she have changed now and want to know her grandchild?

Olivia scooped up the scrapbook and headed toward Matt's

office. She knocked on the open door. Seated behind a desk
with papers spread in front of him, he was talking on the phone.
He had shed his coat and tie, unbuttoned his shirt, rolled up his
sleeves. Her pulse quickened and she wanted to cross the room
and finish unbuttoning his shirt, take it off and run her hands
over his muscled chest. Momentarily, she forgot why she had
come because Matt was a virile, sexy male. When he motioned
her to come in, she tried to stop thinking about his hot kisses
or his hard body.

She sat across the desk from him. As soon as he ended his
call, he asked, "Getting tired of being on your own?"

"Not in the least."

"I'll knock off in just a few minutes and we can swim and
I'll take you into town to dinner."

"Thank you." She went around the desk to place the scrapbook in front of him. Slipping his arm around her waist, he
pulled her down on his lap. She arched her brows at him. "If
they could see us, people would think that we're really in love."

"In just days we'll be husband and wife for real. We might
as well enjoy each other," he said.

"I quite agree," she said softly and leaned forward to kiss
him. He wrapped his arm around her waist again to return her
kiss that swiftly escalated in passion. She wound her arms
around his neck and kissed him hungrily.

His hand slid over her knee and along her thigh. As she
moaned with pleasure, he tugged her T-shirt out of the cutoffs
and slipped his hand beneath her shirt to cup her breast.

"Matt!" she gasped. Desire was a hot flame low inside her.
The seductive onslaught increased as he leaned down to take her
nipple in his mouth. He licked slowly with his tongue, circling
her bud, sucking and biting lightly, a sweet torment that made
her want to spread her legs and give him full access to her.

Winding her fingers in his hair, she pulled his head up so
she could return to kissing him.

His arousal pressed against her thigh and she wanted him
badly. She ran her hands across his broad shoulders, clinging to

him as he cradled her against his shoulder and leaned over her
to kiss her hungrily. She was barely aware of his hands at the
waist of her cutoffs as he unbuttoned and pushed them away. His
hand slid into her lace panties and he touched her intimately.

Desire flashed like fire. Eagerly, she unbuttoned his shirt and
ran her tongue over his flat nipple. His fingers stroked and
rubbed her, creating a stormy friction that escalated swiftly into
a pounding need.

Moving her hips wildly, she twisted against him as he carried
her to an edge. He kissed her, thrusting his tongue deep and then
slowly withdrawing it, to thrust deeply again, mimicking the
act of sex.

Gasping, she cried out, wanting infinitely more of him.
"Matt!" she cried, turning to straddle him while she unfastened
his belt and trousers to free him. She leaned down to take his
thick, throbbing shaft in her mouth.

He closed his eyes and wound his fingers in her hair,
groaning as she licked and caressed him.

He started to slide her over him, but she caught his hands. His
eyes flew open and desire burned in their depths. "Olivia—"

"We can wait until after our wedding. It's not that far away."
She scooted off his lap and pulled on her clothes, straightening them, meeting his hot gaze and turning to walk away from
him. "We're waiting," she said again, as if to convince herself.

When she turned around, he had straightened his clothes and
was sitting watching her with a smoldering gaze.

"This marriage will be good, Matt."

"Yeah, it will," he replied, but she wondered if his thoughts
were on making love instead of what she said to him. "It'll be
hot and sexy," he said in a husky voice that made her wonder
if she could continue to wait until Saturday.

She moved back near him. "I know something we didn't put
in that prenup agreement," she said, leaning one hand on his
desk and bending closer to him.

He looked up at her. "Yeah, what's that?" he asked in a husky
voice while he slid his fingers slowly up her arm to her throat.

"What if we want to give this baby a brother or a sister? If I want to, will that be acceptable to you?"

"Hell, yes, it would. I never dreamed I'd have a child of my own. Shortly after Margo and I married, she made it plain that she was never having children."

"How awful to not tell you until later!" Olivia exclaimed.

"Yeah. We had some real fights over it because before marriage she hadn't leveled with me about not wanting children." He slanted Olivia a look and his blue eyes filled with curiosity. "So if I want another baby, you'll agree to my getting you pregnant?"

"Yes, I will," she said. "I think it would be wonderful to have more than one."

"How many do you want?" he asked and a suspicious note crept into his voice.

"One more child would be marvelous."

"We agree on something."

She laughed. "We haven't disagreed that much. We got through the prenup without too many battles."

"More or less. What's this?" he asked, turning the baby book around. "Damn, I haven't seen this since I was a kid."

"There are baby books for all of you on a shelf in a closet in the library. They were locked in a box."

"I haven't thought about that in years. They were locked away when we were little kids so we couldn't get to them."

"Why didn't your dad want you to look at your baby books?"

"Probably just didn't want us tearing them up. By the time we were big enough to open the box to look at the pictures, I guess none of us wanted to. I never did."

Olivia opened the book and pointed to a picture. "Matt, that's your mother, isn't it?"

"That's her," he said gruffly.

"Where is she now?"

"How the hell should I know? None of us have seen her since we were little kids."

"She'll be our baby's grandmother."

He looked up and his expression was a storm cloud. "Don't get any sentimental ideas."

"She will be the grandmother. How do you know if she hasn't changed in all these years—"

"Dammit, no! Don't you contact her. She walked out on us. Do you know what that does to a little kid?"

"I can well imagine," Olivia answered solemnly, thinking about her own parents who had been a problem all her life.

"We're not contacting her or even trying to if you possibly could. She could live in Australia for all I know."

"You hired a P.I. to check into my background. Why don't you learn her whereabouts and a little about her? She might deplore what she did, Matt."

"No. And don't you even think about it."

"It doesn't matter to you that she's the grandmother?"

"It does not. She wasn't a mother to us. She's not going to be a grandmother to this baby. Understood?"

Even though she mulled over what he said, she nodded.

"Olivia, I mean it. You forget her. She didn't give a damn about us."

"She's beautiful, Matt."

"What's that got to do with anything?"

"Nothing. I just wondered how long since you've even looked at one of her pictures."

"Actually, not for years, nor do I care to now. I would think you'd understand my attitude because of your own background, although I know your parents never abandoned you."

"They might as well have," she said, looking at the window and remembering her own life. Her gaze swung back to Matt. "Very well. She's your mother, so you have the right to ignore her, but you've never heard her side of the story and your father is a strong-willed man."

"Olivia, if you were married and had four little kids, almost babies, would you walk out on them for another man?"

"Of course I wouldn't. You should know that."

"That's right. So what kind of woman abandons her family?"

"I just thought she might have regretted what she did. Or she might have tried to come back and your father wouldn't let her—have you ever thought of that?"

"I don't think so because he was hurt. As young as I was, I know he changed when she left. He's never been as carefree or good-humored since. I don't think he would have kept her away. You just said you wouldn't walk out on little kids."

"I suppose you're right," Olivia said with a sigh as she picked up the scrapbook. He caught her arm.

"Leave the scrapbook and we'll go swim now."

"I'll put it up and meet you at the pool."

"We could shower together before our swim," he suggested, trailing his fingers along her arm. She looked at him with arched eyebrows.

"I think not."

"We're going to be married soon," he replied. She suspected he was teasing her and didn't have any expectations of showering with her.

"Until then, no." She grabbed the scrapbook and left, hearing him chuckle behind her.

Matt watched the sway of her hips as she left his office. He tossed his pen on the desk and thought about his baby pictures with his mother. He didn't like looking back and remembering the hurt and longing.

"Damn, it's been a long time," he said to himself. He didn't want to contact his mother or have Olivia get in touch with her. His thoughts jumped to Olivia and desire stirred. She was sexy, gorgeous and so self-possessed it continually surprised him. Today, she had been cool, decisive and as far as he could tell, got exactly what she wanted in the prenuptial agreement. She didn't seem to care that he put a stipulation in that if they divorced, she forfeited all rights to any money from him except child support. Her attitude toward money was also amazing, but then it always dealt with her losing control of her baby.

Marriage to Olivia. It was far more palatable today than it had been yesterday. Matt strode out of the room, hurrying to change to swim because he looked forward to being with her. At the thought of her long legs and lush body, he broke out in a sweat. He moved faster, longing to get into cool water and put out the fires his imagination ignited.

When he stepped outside, she was there, stretched on a chaise longue with her eyes closed. As he approached her, his gaze ran over her and he marveled again how flat her stomach was. She didn't look one degree pregnant.

Matt was intrigued by her. Olivia was fascinating, unpredictable and he had to admire and respect her and admit that she had gotten the best of him, as well as his dad, in the contests over their futures. Maybe someday he and Olivia would love each other. It surprised him that he even considered the notion. Was her influence changing him?

Olivia had stretched on the chaise to read, but in minutes she'd shoved the book aside and closed her eyes. It was cool and pleasant by the pool. Then she heard the door slide open and she watched Matt who had changed to his brief swim trunks. A white towel was thrown casually over his broad shoulder. Like flint striking a rock, the moment their gazes locked, sparks flew. Olivia's pulse raced and she inhaled deeply. As he approached her, she could see desire heat his blue gaze.

Looking powerful, too appealing, he strolled toward her until he reached the chaise. His gaze left hers and drifted slowly over her, making every inch of her tingle. When he looked into her eyes again, she was breathless, wanting to reach for him.

Stretching out beside her, he drew her into his arms and turned her on her side to face him. Pressed against his hard length with only tiny scraps of material between them, she ached with desire. Each encounter, every hour, her need for him grew. His body was warm, hard. She could feel the rough texture of his thighs with the short dark hairs as her legs pressed against his.

"Let's swim in the nude," he suggested, unfastening her swim top to shove it away and then pushing down the skimpy scrap of material that only partially covered her bottom. With eager, trembling hands, she shoved down his trunks and pressed against his arousal. She twisted away from his kiss. "We're waiting until our wedding night."

"Sure," he whispered gruffly and covered her mouth with his again until she wriggled away and stood.

As she retrieved her suit, he watched her, his eyes taking in every naked inch of her. "I want to kiss you from head to toe and love you until you're senseless," he whispered.

She turned her head to slant him a look. Beneath his watchful gaze, she pulled on her suit. He was stretched back on the chaise, his arousal hard and ready for her. Her heart pounded and she longed to go right back into his arms.

Even though he wasn't touching her, she was in flames. Unable to resist, she walked closer and then she leaned down over him, brushing her breasts against his bare chest and raising slightly to look him straight in the eye. "Next Saturday, I'm going to love you until you're too exhausted to move," she whispered and bent down again to draw a line down his chest with her tongue, sliding lower over his flat, washboard stomach, tasting his slightly salty skin. She looked up. "I want you to want me until you're crazy with desire."

She drew the tip of her tongue lower, over his thick manhood.

He groaned and sat up, sweeping her into his arms to kiss her passionately, pulling her into his embrace. Her heart thudded and she kissed him in a dizzying spiral that momentarily made everything else between them insignificant. Surroundings and circumstances vanished. His kisses changed her to a quivering, boneless mass of jelly. She wanted him as she had never wanted a man. He could drive her to a point of need that made her lose all reason.

"Later, later," she whispered, pulling her top back in place and turning to walk away from him toward the pool.

Without looking back, she went down the steps into the pool, letting the water swirl around her. As she cooled down, her racing pulse slowed to a normal beat. She swam in long strokes, in no hurry, just wanting to relax and cope with scalding desire. And try to get a wall of resistance between Matt and her.

He followed, diving into the water, swimming to catch up with her. He bobbed up beside her and moved them both where they could touch bottom and stand. He slid his arm around her waist to pull her close.

"Next Saturday, you're mine," he said, sliding his hand over her hip.

Her eyebrow arched. "It's mutual that day."

She kicked away from him, and for the next half hour any time he swam close, she turned to swim away. She kept distance between them, enjoying the water, wanting to be in his arms, excited to be with him.

Finally she climbed out. "I'll go dress for dinner," she called, hurrying to slip into her cover-up.

"As far as I'm concerned, you can eat dressed the way you are right now," he said, climbing out behind her. Water splashed off his body and her pulse jumped while she assessed him thoroughly.

She gave him an amused look. "I think I better put some clothes between us," she said and left, her back tingling because she was certain that his gaze followed her across the patio until she was out of his sight.

She let out her breath. By next Saturday night, they would be wild with desire and she intended to make love to him until he never wanted to let her out of his life.

When she returned to the patio, he was in jeans and a fresh T-shirt that clung to his muscles and revealed his powerful shoulders and biceps. Wind lifted locks of his black hair and she thought about how it felt to run her fingers through his thick hair. His gaze drifted over her T-shirt and cutoffs and as she walked up to him, she saw the approving warmth in his eyes.

"You look great," he said.

"Thank you," she answered, smiling at him. "I'm glad you approve."

"I approve except I'd like to peel you out of your T-shirt and cutoffs."

"Maybe later," she said. He smiled, but his eyes sparkled with anticipation that matched her bubbling excitement.

While a thin column of gray smoke drifted skyward, steaks sizzled on the grill. The tantalizing smell whetted her appetite. "I'm starving," she said.

"The feeling is mutual," he said in such a husky voice, she turned to look at him. "I could eat you for dinner," he said, and her pulse jumped.

"No, that comes later," she replied softly, and his chest expanded as he inhaled.

"I'm ready to cool down with some tea," she said, seeing that he had two glasses of iced tea poured. He handed one to her and in minutes they sat at the table with thick steaks and baked potatoes.

"Here's to our future together," he said, raising his glass of iced tea and she touched her glass against his with a faint clink.

"May it be less stormy than our past," she added, and he smiled. "Soon I'll enroll in the university for the fall. It's a dream come true for me to be able to do that. I'll carry a full course load. Thank you, Matt, for your generosity."

"I have to thank you in return. I'm getting a baby in my life."

"You'll be a good dad, I imagine."

He shrugged. "I don't know until I try and see how I do. At least I'll love the little boy or girl."

"Now that the prenup agreement is out of the way, I need to concentrate on the wedding arrangements. The wedding planner will be here in the morning at ten."

"All that is up to you. I'll take care of the honeymoon arrangements," he said.

"We're taking a honeymoon?" she asked, surprised. "I'm amazed we're going on a honeymoon."

"Why not take a honeymoon?" he asked and the corner of his mouth lifted slightly.

"Since we're not in love—"

"We're going to have great sex," he said, lowering his voice and leaning closer, leaving his steak untouched. "I want you all to myself. Super sex is a good reason for a honeymoon."

"I suppose," she said, but she had a pang of longing for more than lust and great sex. She wanted a honeymoon where they cared about each other, but she knew that wasn't going to be the situation and she better not delude herself. "I like surprises," she said carefully.

"Good. You'll have to wait until next Saturday to find out where we'll honeymoon."

She laughed, and he drew his finger along her cheek. "I like your laughter, Olivia. We're going to have a workable arrangement."

As she gazed into his blue eyes, desire filled his expression. She put down her fork and got up, walking around to him to sit in his lap. When she approached him, he pushed back his chair and the moment she sat down he wrapped his arms around her.

"I intend for it to be better than a 'workable arrangement,'" she said. She leaned forward to kiss him, sliding her tongue into his mouth and drawing it slowly over his. His arms went around her and he held her close, kissing her hard until she leaned back.

"How's that for 'workable'?" she whispered. "Or this?" she asked, tugging up his T-shirt so she could slide her tongue over his flat nipple and then shed kisses lower. "Or this?" she asked.

"Dammit," he said, winding his fingers in her hair and tilting her head back to give him full access to her mouth. He bent over her, molding her to him. His hand cupped her body, pulling her hips closer while he kissed her.

She pushed against him and twisted away and they gazed at each other. "It'll be workable, all right," she said, sliding off his lap and standing. "And we're waiting because it won't be many more days."

He stood to embrace her. "You're going to be mine, Olivia," he said in a raspy voice that played like a soft wind across her raw nerves.

"Be warned, Matt. Soon I may find your heart, and it'll be mine."

His eyes clouded and his jaw firmed. "You're a romantic, a

dreamer and an optimist. Watch out because I don't want to hurt you. What we're going to have will be great, but it won't be love."

She smiled at him, hiding the stab of pain his words caused and surprised by the intensity of hurt. "We'll see," she said, wondering if she was deluding herself about him. What would it take to make him fall in love with her?

"In the meantime, let's clear things up and sit down and do some wedding planning," she said, trying to keep her voice light and casual.

Matt's cell phone rang and he pulled it out of his pocket to answer. "It's Nick," he whispered. "Hi," he said. "I've got news and I know this is short notice. Olivia Brennan and I want you to come home next weekend. We're getting married."

Olivia walked away to give Matt privacy even though he was quiet and his brother had to be doing all the talking. She wondered if Nick was trying to talk Matt out of marrying her. Olivia picked up dishes to carry them to the kitchen. She knew his family didn't want him to marry her. Was she insisting on something that was going to be a disaster for all concerned, and most of all, for her?

She knew she better decide for certain because next Saturday would soon be here.

Friday evening a week later, Olivia had another attack of butterflies. Within the hour Matt's brother was arriving and in an hour and a half his sister would get in. The wedding planner had assistants getting the house ready and tonight they would have a rehearsal and then all go to Rincon to a country club for dinner. The closer the wedding, the more nervous Olivia became, assailed with doubts and last-minute jitters. Was she doing the right thing? she asked herself for what seemed like the hundredth time. Yet she was falling in love with Matt and she prayed that with this marriage, love would come to him. Then doubts would bombard her. Was she locking herself into a loveless union that would grow more difficult with time?

If she thought about walking out, though, she knew that wasn't what she wanted to do.

She slipped her red dress over her head, feeling the silky lining that was cool against her skin. Her wispy underclothes were red lace, a luxury she'd never before been able to afford. She looked around the bedroom and was reassured by the life she was giving her baby.

The moment she walked into the family room and looked at Matt in a charcoal suit and red tie, her qualms fled. When his blue eyes met her gaze, her heart thudded and her concerns about marriage vanished.

Another tall, handsome man stood beside him and they both crossed the room to her. "Olivia, meet my brother, Nick."

Extending her hand, she looked at a man with curly brown hair who stood an inch taller than Matt, as broad through the shoulders with the same straight nose and firm jaw. There the resemblances ended. Nick's dark brown eyes flashed with curiosity as she shook his hand.

"Welcome to the family," Nick said and smiled, his teeth looking a dazzling white against his dark tan.

"Thank you," she replied, relieved that he was friendly because Matt's father still was not and he had declined to join them tonight. "I'm glad you could get here and be with us for the wedding."

"Wouldn't have missed it," Nick said. "Now if we can just get my wandering sister home. Dad will come around eventually."

Unable to agree with him, Olivia nodded, but she didn't want to say so.

"Ahh, here she is," Matt said, looking over Olivia's head. She turned to see a tall, striking blonde in a sleeveless beige silk dress.

"I think all three of you had different mothers," Olivia remarked to Matt and he flashed a grin. "You don't look alike at all."

Without answering her, he was gone, crossing the room in long strides with his brother as both of them welcomed their sister. Olivia watched them hug and kiss, thinking all three could have been models. But then Duke Ransome was a handsome man and Olivia remembered the pictures in Matt's baby book of his mother who had been stunning. Why wouldn't their offspring be handsome and beautiful?

Matt approached her with his sister and brother. "Olivia, meet my sister, Katherine. Katherine, this is my fiancée, Olivia Brennan."

Gazing into crystal-blue eyes, Olivia smiled and shook Katherine's hand.

"So you're the woman who has shaken up this family? As least it put an end to mourning Jeff so much because now there's a new worry."

"And I'm the new worry?" Olivia asked with amusement.

Suddenly Katherine smiled. "I believe you are, but maybe it's not warranted. Goodness knows, this family can use new blood. And a baby is fantastic! I was beginning to give up on ever having a baby in our midst. You two didn't help the cause," she teased, looking at first Matt and then Nick.

"I don't see you helping the cause either," Matt told her in a good-natured tone.

"Don't ever hold your breath on that one," Katherine responded, turning her attention back to Olivia. "So you're going to law school?"

Olivia nodded. "I have to get my undergrad degree first." All the time she talked to Matt's brother and sister, she was aware of Matt at her side. He was friendly enough, but it should be obvious to everyone that he wasn't in love.

Within the hour the wedding party and the minister arrived and they went through a rehearsal. While they received instructions, Olivia felt a pang over the sham marriage. Yet each time she was besieged with qualms, she looked at Matt and knew she was making the best possible choice. If only…she blanked that out. Tomorrow she would be Mrs. Matthew Ransome, for better or for worse. How she wished she had his love.

As soon as they finished the brief rehearsal, they left for the Rincon country club and a catered barbecue dinner.

It was midnight before they returned to the ranch. Nick and

Katherine were staying at their father's house, so they told Matt and Olivia good-night and drove on down the road.

As Olivia walked across the porch and into the house, Matt draped his arm across her shoulders.

"Your brother and sister were wonderful to me. The way they treated me, you'd think we were in love and having a real marriage."

"Nick and Katherine are all right."

"I'm sorry for your sake that your father hasn't had a change of heart."

They entered the kitchen where only one small light was on. Matt turned to face her and put his hands on her shoulders. "Dad doesn't change easily, and he thinks I'm getting into something that's going to make me unhappy."

"I hope that isn't the case," she said, "and I'm truly sorry that he didn't join us. I know it was difficult for the three of you without him present."

"Oh, no. Dad just cut himself out of an evening with all of us. He'll be there tomorrow. You'll see."

She doubted it, but at the moment she was far more aware of Matt running his hands along her arms up to her shoulders.

"Your brother and sister were really great. I wish they stayed here."

"Got butterflies?" he asked, changing the subject abruptly and looking intently at her.

"Not badly," she replied, not wanting to admit how bad a case of nerves she had.

"C'mon. We'll sit in the kitchen and have hot chocolate. Or we could do something else," he said, leaning down to brush her lips with his.

Her heart thudded, but she held him away. "Until tomorrow night," she whispered and stood on tiptoe to kiss him long and passionately.

Finally she twisted away and gazed at him. "I'll pass on the hot chocolate and see you in the morning," she said.

She went upstairs to her room and closed the door.

Tomorrow she would get married to a man who didn't love her. She shook her head. Every time she questioned herself about the ceremony, she knew she wanted to go through with it.

The next morning Olivia could hardly believe that the time had come. This day she would become Mrs. Matthew Ransome. She still half expected his father to do something to stop the wedding.

When Olivia entered the kitchen for breakfast, she heard a knock at the back door and opened it to face Katherine who was in a T-shirt and cutoffs with her hair caught up in a clip. She carried a dress bag and Olivia knew it held the dress that Katherine would wear as one of her attendants.

"Come in. I was just starting to fix breakfast, so why don't you join me?" Olivia asked.

"Sure. That's why I came and left the men behind. Matt can go join them if he wants." She followed Olivia into the kitchen. "I'll hang up my dress in a bedroom," she said, carrying a yellow sheath encased in a clear bag.

In minutes she returned and looked around. "What can I do?"

"I guess fix coffee if you want some. Or pour orange juice."

As Katherine got out the coffeepot, she glanced at Olivia. "So no cold feet?"

"No. Maybe a few jitters, but I'm delighted with our agreement and I think we can make a good marriage of this union."

Katherine continued to study Olivia. "Just don't break my brother's heart. He's already been through that once."

"I have no intention of hurting him," Olivia replied. "Just the opposite is much more likely to happen."

Katherine's brows arched. "You're in love with my brother?"

Olivia could feel her cheeks flush. "I'm beginning to care about him," she replied cautiously.

Katherine nodded, looking lost in thought. "Well then, I hope you both fall in love. Whatever happens, I hope you have a good arrangement. I don't want to see Matt hurt. I don't want to see you hurt." Katherine studied Olivia. "I watched you two last night. You may be good for my brother."

Olivia smiled. "I hope I am," she replied, wondering if Katherine had ever been in love. Matt had talked very little about his brother or sister. She broke eggs into a skillet and stirred them. "We've been so busy all week making wedding arrangements and getting a prenuptial agreement finished that we haven't had a chance to talk about much else."

"Matt's reliable and he keeps his word," Katherine said. "And we're all thrilled about the baby. You don't look pregnant in the least."

"I definitely am," Olivia said, remembering that Jeff wasn't thrilled and hated learning that he would be a father, but she saw no point in telling Katherine. She dropped slices of bread into a toaster and returned to scrambling the eggs. In a few minutes she sat at the table across from Katherine.

"Olivia, Matt told me what Dad offered you."

"Your father may never like me or speak to me."

"He'll come around when your baby is born. That took some guts to stand up to him and it took something special to turn him down."

"You'd have turned him down, wouldn't you, Katherine?" Olivia asked, suddenly certain that Katherine would have.

"Yes. I wouldn't give up a baby of mine for money. I'm glad you didn't either. You may be really good for our family."

"Thanks," Olivia said, feeling as if she had found a friend she could trust in Matt's sister.

"Good morning," Matt said, striding into the kitchen, his gaze going to Olivia as he crossed the room to her and leaned down to brush a light kiss on her lips. He squeezed her shoulder lightly. "Do you want to get married today?" he asked, smiling at her.

"Yes, I do. I hope you're not having second thoughts," she said.

"Nope. Not at all." He turned to his sister. "Good morning, Kat," he said, crossing the kitchen to get toast and eggs.

"You can join Dad and Nick at Dad's house," she said and Matt set down the plate he held.

"I'll go do that and leave you ladies to your wedding talk." He winked at Olivia and left the room.

Katherine turned a speculative gaze on Olivia. "Maybe you're closer to Matt loving you than you think."

Olivia merely nodded because she knew she was a long way from having his love now.

By the time she and Katherine had finished breakfast and she had showed Katherine her wedding dress, the wedding planner and entourage arrived followed by the caterer and soon the house bustled with people. Katherine left to dress and in minutes Olivia's friends who would be attendants arrived to help her.

The band arrived and while they set up on the patio, Katherine joined Olivia and Olivia's friends who would be attendants.

Still caught in a dreamlike quality, Olivia dressed in the white silk. She wore white rosebuds in her hair, which was pinned on top of her head with a few locks tumbling free. Looking at herself in the mirror, she couldn't keep from staring, dazed by her reflection. Her wedding day. Marriage to Matt.

"You look beautiful," Katherine said with a cloudy look in her eyes, and Olivia wondered what had happened to Katherine in the past.

The moment was gone and it was time for the ceremony to begin.

Folding chairs had been placed in the large living room and banks of white roses were placed along the walls. As the piano player began, the groomsmen and the bridegroom entered the front of the room. Then the bridesmaids went down the aisle and finally, with a flourish of a trumpeter, Olivia knew it was time for her to proceed.

The guests stood, turning toward her. While her heart drummed, she walked with Nick who would accompany her down the aisle and then take his place beside Matt as best man.

She saw only Matt, whose blue-eyed gaze was locked with hers. And then she began walking down the aisle toward him.

Ten

Matt's blue eyes bored into her. Tall and devastatingly handsome in his black tux, he smiled at her. She smiled in return while her heart raced.

She was barely aware when Nick moved away after placing her hand in Matt's. His strong, warm fingers closed around her hand and they faced the minister.

She watched Matt as she repeated her vows. His blue eyes were brilliant, yet she couldn't guess what he was thinking—whether he was happy or angry now that the moment was actually here and he was making what they had planned to be a lifetime commitment.

"I, Olivia, take thee, Matt, to be my lawful, wedded husband," she said, dazzled by what was happening. She was marrying Matt Ransome. It was real. The whole marriage agreement had seemed a dream until this moment, but now it was coming true.

Then they were finished and the minister introduced them to the guests as Mr. and Mrs. Matthew Ransome.

"You may kiss the bride," he said to Matt and she looked up as Matt slipped his arms lightly around her and leaned close. His lips brushed hers and then were firm as they met hers in a way that seemed as binding to her heart as the vows they had just spoken. Her heart thudded and the amazement of actually being married to him rocked her. When he released her, she opened her eyes to find him watching her. He smiled and enveloped her hand in his before they turned. Hurrying beside him, she still tingled from his kiss.

As they walked up the aisle, she looked at the guests. With his jaw clamped shut Duke Ransome stared at her. He appeared as angry as he had the last time she had seen him, but her happiness was a solid wall around her emotions this day. Matt whisked her through the house to circle back to the living room for pictures.

Dressed in the pale yellow silk sheath, Katherine walked up to hug her lightly. "Welcome to our family, Mrs. Ransome," she said and smiled at Olivia.

"Thanks, Katherine. I intend for this union to last," Olivia said and Katherine nodded.

"If you ever want to talk, just call me. I know Matt pretty well. Give him time. He was hurt badly before."

Olivia nodded.

"Welcome, Olivia," Nick said, hugging her, his brown eyes twinkling. "I hope for the very best for both of you. May your future be grand."

"Thanks, Nick. You and Katherine were great to drop everything and come home on such short notice."

"I wouldn't have missed this for anything," Katherine said with a smile. Then Matt was beside her again and Katherine turned to hug him.

"You be good to her, y'hear," she said, poking her brother in the chest with her finger.

"What else would I be?" he asked Katherine with a smile.

"Bride and groom, please," the photographer called and they broke up, stepping back as Olivia and Matt posed for the first picture. As Olivia stood with Matt's arm around her waist, she saw Duke watching from the far side of the room, a scowl still on his face. Was he going to give her trouble in the future, she wondered. Then she forgot him as the photographer began giving her instructions on a pose for the next picture.

It was half an hour before they joined the guests on the patio for the reception. She unfastened and removed her train and in minutes Matt removed his coat. The sunny morning would be carved in her memory forever, more garlands of white roses, the tempting smell of roasting beef and pork, and a crowd of friends of Matt and his family. The band played, the splash of the fountain added to the festive ambience. Yet surroundings and friends faded from her notice when Olivia looked at her handsome husband.

She gazed across the patio at him as he laughed at something one of his friends said. Tall, rugged and handsome, he took her breath. The week had drawn them closer—or had she been the only one to feel that way? Would she ever look at him without a jump in her pulse?

As she watched him, he turned his head and gazed into her eyes and even across the crowd and space that separated them, sparks flew. He watched her, yet he was talking to the man beside him. Without taking his gaze from hers, Matt laughed and said something to his friend. As she watched, Matt crossed the patio and strolled toward her.

With each step closer, her pulse accelerated. He stopped only inches away, smiling down at her with that crooked, inviting smile that made her weak in the knees.

"Hi, Mrs. Ransome."

"I don't know if I'll ever become accustomed to that."

"You will someday. You look gorgeous, Olivia," he said seriously.

"Thank you. You look rather nice yourself."

"Thanks," he said and touched a lock of her hair. "I'm about ready to leave."

"We can't leave now!" she exclaimed. "Not with all these

friends you have and your sister and brother here. We have to stay for an hour or two at least."

The corner of his mouth lifted in a smile, but she could see desire burning in his blue eyes. "The very first moment we can get out of here without being rude, you come get me. Promise?"

"All right, I will. In the meantime, we should circulate." Before she could say anything else, well-wishers came up and Matt introduced her to three of his friends who were friendly, polite and respectful and made her realize how much her life had already changed.

When the band director announced that the groom would have the first dance with the bride, Matt turned her into his arms as the band began to play. He held her close, her hand wrapped in his with her other hand on his broad shoulder. He was clean-shaven, his hair slightly windblown now, so handsome she couldn't stop staring.

"I think time has stopped. I've been waiting forever to get you off to myself."

She smiled. "Not a lot longer."

"I could whisk you away after this dance," he said.

"No, you can't. We have to cut the cake and talk to more guests. Patience, patience."

"What saves me is the realization that it's going to be worth the wait," he drawled in a deep voice and she gave him another smile.

"Soon enough we will be naked in bed together and you'll forget how long you had to wait."

He inhaled deeply and his eyes darkened. "That just makes me want to get out of here more than ever."

"Think about something else." She tilted her head to study him. "I don't even know what you like to do for entertainment or what you want out of life."

"Right now, it's you."

Laughing, she glanced across the patio to see his father talking to a group of men. Duke Ransome laughed at something one of the men said to him.

"I see your father has loosened up."

"He's already had a couple of drinks so that took off the edge and now he's with some of his cronies. He's not thinking about us. At this point, it's a done deal. He'll probably settle back and accept life the way it is. When the baby comes, you'll wonder if he's the same man you know now. He'll be nuts about this grandchild."

"That's what Katherine said."

"As a matter of fact, don't be surprised if he doesn't appear with a peace offering. I heard him talking to Katherine and I think he's beginning to plan on having a couple of rooms in his house redone for a nursery and a playroom."

She glanced again at Duke. "I'll believe it when I see it. He predicted disaster if I married you and he wanted desperately to run me off."

"You'll see. He'll thaw fast now because you're family."

She looked up at Matt. "Family. That's one of the most wonderful things anyone has ever said to me."

He laughed and spun her around. His arm tightened around her waist to hold her close while they danced.

"Everyone is watching," she said.

"That's because you're beautiful."

"Thank you, but I don't think that's why." She clung to him, following his lead and thought they danced as if they had been dancing together for years. He twirled her around again and then pulled her close and she smiled up at him. He gazed down with a hungry look that increased her heartbeat. She wrapped her arms around his neck and danced with him, smiling up at him.

"This is going to be a good marriage," he said.

"Trying to convince yourself?" she asked, feeling a bubbling undercurrent of excitement.

"I think it will be good. Don't you?"

"I hope so, but who knows what the future will bring? You and I barely know each other."

He looked over her head. "I think we've got everyone convinced otherwise, except my family and whoever you've told."

The band finished and commenced a slow number. She heard a deep voice behind her.

"May I have this dance?"

She turned to face Nick, who glanced at his brother. "Get lost," he said to Matt and took her in his arms lightly.

"I'm glad you came for the wedding and Matt is glad to see you," she said, looking into his dark brown eyes and marveling how different the brothers looked.

"I wanted to come see for myself. I don't want my brother hurt," Nick said solemnly. "I didn't have a chance to talk to you alone last night. Don't hurt him, Olivia. He said that the two of you aren't in love, but seeing you together last night made me feel better."

"I don't intend to hurt him. I hope neither one of us hurts the other," she said, looking up at Nick. "Matt was the one who approached me and who wanted my baby in the Ransome family. Always remember that. I didn't come to your family or ask your family for money."

"I know. Matt told me that Jeff didn't want his baby. That's sad news for the rest of us. We need this baby in our family. I'm not the marrying kind. Jeff is gone. God knows, Katherine won't marry. Matt keeps his heart under lock and key. Your baby is the only hope for the next generation for our family."

"That's sort of a bleak outlook about you and Katherine and Matt."

"Nope. That's just the way it is. Just be good to him. He'll be good to you."

"I'm glad to hear that," she replied.

"You ever want to talk, you can call me."

"Thanks. Katherine made the same offer."

"In spite of us traveling and not seeing each other constantly, we're all close. We care about each other."

"Good. That's important."

He spun around and she saw Matt standing in a group of people while he watched her dance.

Matt dimly heard the conversation going on beside him, but

his attention was on Olivia. She was gorgeous today. As she had walked down the aisle, he thought his heart would pound out of his chest. She still exuded that earthy, sexy air, but today, she was stunning. He couldn't stop watching her, devouring her with his gaze and wanting her in his arms more than ever. He had made a bargain that just got better with each day. It was a loveless marriage of convenience, but it was a fantastic arrangement in a lot of ways and one of them was the sex he was going to have with Olivia.

His temperature climbed at the thought and he tried to focus on what was being said by friends. In minutes though, his attention was right back on his new wife. He glanced at his watch. He couldn't wait to get her out of here and off to himself.

They hadn't even cut the cake yet and the afternoon threatened to drag on forever. He suspected she was enjoying herself because her eyes sparkled and her face was flushed and she continually smiled.

He was tempted to get her away from Nick to dance with her himself, but he curbed the impulse, even though he ached to hold her. Was she becoming important to him? The notion surprised him because he didn't expect that to happen.

It was only a short leap from being essential to him to being in love with her. Was she going to slip past the barriers around his heart?

In the brief time she had known them she had charmed his brother and sister.

His gaze ran over Olivia in the long, white dress and he imagined her without it, his mouth going dry and his temperature rising again. He glanced at his watch. Time seemed to stand still. He realized the number was ending and he could go claim his bride from his brother.

He threaded his way past couples who wished him well and congratulated him and wanted to talk and finally he was there behind her and he couldn't resist reaching for her.

"Olivia."

When Olivia heard her name, she turned as Matt slipped his

arm around her waist and pulled her close against him. Katherine approached them.

"Come on, you two, before you start dancing again. They're ready for you to cut the cake and the photographer is waiting."

"Gladly," Matt said and Olivia laughed as he took her hand and they followed Katherine across the patio.

Olivia was aware of Matt's hand lightly on hers as they cut into the seven-tier cake together. She had been as dazzled by the cake as all the other details of this wedding where cost was not a problem. The entire day had seemed a dream and she couldn't get used to being Mrs. Matt Ransome. She looked up at her handsome new husband and felt a pang. Only one thing was missing to make the day perfect, but that one thing was the most important of all.

It was three in the afternoon when Matt found her. "We can get out of here now," he said, taking her arm. She smiled at him.

"Let's tell everyone goodbye," she said, and waved at his sister. He groaned and followed her across the patio to Katherine where she stood by the pool.

"We're leaving, Katherine. Thanks so much for coming for the wedding. You take care of yourself," he said and hugged his sister.

"You, too, Matt. I'm happy for you and I hope this works out for you and Olivia."

She turned to hug Olivia. "Be patient with my brother," she said, giving a toss of her head that sent her blond hair swirling across her shoulders. Olivia smiled.

"I'll try. Thanks for coming, Katherine. It meant a lot and I'm so glad to get to know you," Olivia said.

"Hey, I want a hug, too," Nick said, joining them and turning to Olivia who hugged him lightly.

"Thanks for coming to the wedding and I'm glad to meet you, Nick."

"We're happy to have you in the family, Olivia. You're the best thing that's happened to us in years and years."

"I hope so," she replied, wondering how long Nick would feel that way and wondering how much Matt shared the sentiment.

Matt embraced Katherine and then as the two brothers hugged, Matt thanked Nick for coming again. "Don't wait so long to come home, you two," he said to both of them. "Now we're getting the hell out of Dodge," he said, taking Olivia's arm and striding across the patio to a back gate. She stretched out her legs to keep up with him, her excitement mounting.

"I have a car stashed out here. A plane is waiting and we're on our way."

The moment they were in the car she turned to him. "Where are we going? You have to tell me now."

"To Ariel."

"I've never heard of it. Where is that?"

"It's a tiny island off the Yucatan Peninsula. I own it. When I bought the place, it already had a name, but it's not big enough for you to have ever heard of it. We have an airstrip on Ariel so I can fly in and out of there. It's isolated, peaceful and beautiful. I think you'll like it. I have a staff who keep it maintained when I'm there. They were there all last week getting everything ready, but we'll have the house to ourselves. Two couples live on the island who work for me and they'll come in to clean and cook part of the time."

"Aren't they isolated out there by themselves?"

"They like living there and have their own planes on the island. The Thorensons are retired stockbrokers doing just what they want. The demands of the job I hired them for aren't great. The other couple, the Ellisons, had their own business that went belly up, and they've said this job is perfect. A small paradise and a plane to get them out of there whenever they want. So far we've been fortunate during hurricane seasons. We've been hit, but most structures have weathered the storms. I've had to replace roofs and windows, but it's been worth it. You'll see."

She stared at him, amazed that he would own an island. He glanced at her. "You're staring."

"You just surprise me."

He smiled. "Good, because you've been one surprise after

another to me. We're all amazed you turned down my dad—
by all, I mean Nick and Katherine and me."

"Katherine said now that she knows me a little, she wasn't
so surprised. And she said she understood. She would have
turned him down."

"Katherine probably would, but that's different. Katherine
is unpredictable. She's grown up with a life of ease and wealth
and what she wanted, most of the time. Not so with you. You've
had a life of poverty and hardship. That should make my dad's
offer much more attractive and far more difficult to resist."

"No, it didn't. I didn't have to think about it."

"Nick couldn't imagine you turning so much down because
he had the same impression I did until I told him about you and
our first meeting. They like you."

While he talked, Olivia ran her hand over the elegant leather
seat and was amazed how swiftly her life had changed. Never had
she dreamed of living the life she was now. Even more astound-
ing was her handsome new husband. As she studied his profile,
her mouth went dry. She wanted to touch him and kiss him.

"How long?" she asked in a breathless, throaty voice that
made him glance at her and then back to his driving.

"How long *what?*"

"How long until we're on that island and alone?" she asked
softly, sliding her hand along his muscled thigh.

His fingers wrapped around hers tightly. "Not soon enough,"
he replied and his voice thickened. While he watched his
driving, he raised her hand to brush a kiss along her knuckles.

They sped to the airport in Fort Worth and soon were aboard
the Ransome jet.

When they reached cruising speed and she could move
around the plane, she unbuckled her seat belt. "I'll change out
of this dress."

"Just stay the way you are," Matt said, catching her wrist.
"We'll be there before you know it."

She sat back and buckled up again. "All right, but will I step
off the plane into sand?"

"Nope, and you can hold up your skirt. I've got a high wall around my place so soon you can go completely naked and no one will see you except me which is exactly what I intend. That's one reason I bought this particular island. Privacy and peace and I can get to it quickly and easily."

Olivia looked below at the lush green fields and then she turned back to her husband.

"Your dad congratulated me on my marriage to you today," she said.

"I saw him talking to you and would have joined you if I'd thought you needed to be rescued, but after last week, I know you can hold your own with my dad."

"I think he's just making the most of a bad situation right now."

"He'll accept you. He probably has more respect for you than he did before."

She laughed. "Like father, like son. All of you must have thought your brother got tangled with a real bimbo."

"It was easy to jump to conclusions and make hasty judgments."

"Just remember that in the future," she said, thinking again about the scrapbook of pictures of his mother. "I think there's a remote possibility you might have done that concerning your mother."

His smile vanished, and he leaned forward, catching her chin in his hand. "You leave that alone, Olivia. You're getting into something that doesn't concern you and none of us wants any contact with her. She walked out on us. Get it?"

"Yes, I do, but it was decades ago and the little I've seen of your father, you could have been told a twisted version of the truth. After all, you were little kids. How difficult would it be to bend the truth and convince all of you that you were hearing facts?"

"If you didn't know me and we weren't married, would you try to cultivate my dad's friendship because he's the grandfather of your baby?"

Startled, she gazed at Matt while she mulled over his question and she shook her head. "No, I wouldn't."

"All right. She may be a hell of a lot worse than Dad. Leave it alone. At least my dad raised all of us and he cares deeply about this grandbaby."

She could see Matt's point and she nodded. She smiled at him and leaned forward to place her hands on his knees and brush a kiss lightly on his lips. "Let's not have any cross words mar this day that has been a dream-come-true event so far. It's perfect, Matt, and I want to make you smile and then I want to kiss and love you until you will never want to let me go."

"Do tell, Mrs. Ransome," he drawled softly, leaning inches from her face. "Sounds like the best plan possible to me. We'll have our own private beach and we can stay naked. Food is already cooked, and no one is coming in to do anything unless I call and ask them to." His voice lowered while he drew his finger along the V of her neckline, stirring tingles. "I'm going to love you senseless, Olivia. I feel as if I've been waiting forever for this night."

He slipped his hand behind her head and kissed her long and passionately. As he started to unbuckle her seat belt to pick her up, she caught his hands to stop him and she pulled away. "Wait. Not here and not now."

He looked amused as he leaned back. "I'll wait, but no one is going to disturb us here."

"Just wait until we're alone."

"It already seems like I've waited eons."

She smiled at him and nodded in agreement.

When they began to fly over the Gulf, she looked out at bright blue water with an occasional boat creating a white wake. She spotted a dazzling white cruise ship and pointed each thing out to him even though he was right beside her and could see for himself.

She knew when they approached the island and at first she was astounded how small it looked but when the plane lost altitude to land, she forgot size. Her breath caught and she stared in wonder at white sand that was as dazzling in the sunshine as the cruise ship had been. Palms swayed gently and the water was a brilliant blue, lapping at the shore with tiny whitecaps. She saw the landing strip and two planes tied down and a hangar with a tin roof.

The pilot helped Matt transfer their bags to the waiting car and then Matt held the door for her. As she watched him stride around the car, she knew she was hopelessly in love with him already.

He was too sexy, too appealing, too handsome, too generous, too likeable to keep her heart sealed away. When he circled the car, wind blew locks of his black hair. How had she ever thought she could resist falling in love with him?

Sliding into the car beside her, he leaned over to brush another light kiss on her lips. "Welcome to Ariel, Mrs. Ransome."

"Thank you, Mr. Ransome," she said, trying to keep from being too solemn and losing the joy and excitement she had experienced all day, yet it was sobering to face that fact that she was in love with her virile new husband and know that he not only did not love her in return, but he might not ever stop guarding his heart.

She had locked herself into a loveless marriage. She reminded herself that this loveless marriage was going to be a far better future than she had ever dreamed of before.

She clung to that thought as they swept along a road that was made of broken shells with lush green jungle crowding them.

They rounded a bend and drove into a clearing and her heart jumped at the beauty of the house. Made of white stucco, it was a sharp contrast with the blue waters beyond it. The lawn was well tended with palms and masses of bright red hibiscus, a blooming yellow poui, red chenille plants and masses of pink oleander. Climbing yellow bougainvillea ran up porch columns and over the roof.

"It's paradise, Matt!" she gasped.

"Good. I think so, too, and I'm glad you like it. Wait until you see our ranch in Argentina. We're going to stay here four days and then fly to the ranch."

"Argentina?"

"When I met you, I told you we were buying another

ranch—it's in Argentina. We've leased it for the past five years so it won't be new to our family."

He parked and came around to open the door. As she stepped out, Matt swept her into his arms. Shrieking with surprise, she wrapped her arms around his neck.

"I'll carry my bride over the threshold," he said, going up the steps easily and crossing the porch to enter a house with a wide hallway and a gleaming plank floor. Ceiling fans turned lazily. Matt carried her to the bedroom where he slowly lowered her, letting her slide down his muscled body while he set her on her feet.

"Oh, this is fantastic!" she said, looking through floor-to-ceiling glass doors that opened onto a flower-and-palm-covered patio. White sand ran a hundred yards down to the water.

"You're what's fantastic," he said, catching her wrist and pulling her to him. Removing her veil, he tossed it aside and tugged pins out of her hair. When her hair tumbled over her shoulders, he wound his fingers in it, then tightened his fist and tilted her head to give him access to her mouth.

Her heart thudded, and she forgot their glorious surroundings.

"You're the most beautiful bride in the whole world," he said softly right behind her as he brushed a kiss on her nape and then turned her to face him. "I've been waiting for this moment far too long," he said and his voice lowered another notch.

Eleven

Olivia trembled at the sight of the blatant desire in Matt's intense gaze that lowered to her mouth and made her lips tingle. She stood on tiptoe, wrapping her arms around his neck and pulling him closer while she brushed her lips across his mouth.

With a groan he leaned down. "You'll never know how much I want you," he said, grinding out the words. His arm circled her waist, and he pulled her against him while his mouth covered hers. His tongue stroked hers, sending streaks of fire in its wake. Desire became a white-hot need as she thrust her hips against him.

Kissing her deeply, he leaned over her. Her heart thundered, drowning the sounds of the waves on the beach. She wound her fingers in his hair at his nape and then let her hand slide down to twist free the studs on his shirt. She leaned back to catch his wrist. While she watched him intently, she removed a cuff link so he could slip off his shirt. "I've waited all week, Matt," she whispered.

"I've waited a lifetime. You're what a man fantasizes and dreams about."

"I don't know that I want to be anyone's fantasy," she whispered. "I want you to desire me because I'm Olivia—my own person. One way or another, Matt, I'll get to you. You can't guard your heart against love. You may not be able to guard it against my loving. We'll see." She picked up his other wrist to remove that cuff link. He caressed her nape with his free hand and as soon as she had his shirt off, she tossed it aside.

She drank in the sight of his muscled chest, running her hands over him lightly. "I could look at and touch you forever," she whispered, trembling, on fire with longing, yet wanting to savor every moment of this night. She leaned forward to kiss his nipple while she continued to explore his chest and smooth back with her fingers.

He inhaled deeply and tangled his fingers in her hair. "Ahh, Olivia. You'll burn me to a crisp," he whispered. "I've wanted you since the first moment I saw you."

She leaned down, tracing the tip of her tongue across his flat stomach above his belt while she unfastened his belt and pushed away his trousers.

His hands slipped beneath her arms to pull her up and they looked into each other's eyes, his hungry desire blasting into her like a whirlwind. He hauled her into his embrace, holding her tightly and leaning over her while he kissed her.

In minutes or hours—time was gone and she had no idea, he turned her around and drew his tongue along her nape. His breath was warm, sexy.

He brushed his hands so lightly across the front of her dress and she gasped, feeling the faint contact on her sensitive nipples.

She inhaled and closed her eyes, reaching behind her to slide her hands along his strong thighs.

Cool air spilled across her shoulders and down her back when he unzipped her wedding dress. It fell around her ankles with a swish of silk that she barely noticed, but she was awed to see that his fingers trembled as he turned her to face him.

His burning gaze consumed her as he pushed away the

white scrap of lacy panties she wore and the thigh-high dark hose. He rested his hands on her hips and looked at her in a gaze so filled with need, it was like fingers drifting down over her and caressing her. Then he cupped her breasts, his thumbs circling her nipples leisurely in an exquisite torment that made her clutch his arms and close her eyes and try to draw him closer.

. "You're beautiful!" he said in a raspy voice. "So responsive. So beautiful."

"Matt! I want you," she gasped, trembling with desire and melting from his touch. When he covered her mouth with his, kissing her hard, she shoved down his briefs. His strong arm banded her, pulling her against his hard length.

With a desperate hunger for his loving, she moaned softly, wanting all of him now. His thick shaft pressed against her belly, hot and hard for her. He picked her up while he continued to kiss her and carried her to the bed where he placed his knee and lowered her.

While she wound her arms around his neck, his hands were everywhere, exploring her body with a thoroughness that heightened her insatiable need.

His tongue traced from her ear to her breasts and he took a nipple into his mouth to bite lightly. His tongue drew slow, hot wet circles in a delicious torment around her taut bud. At the same time, he caressed her other breast, stroking her in a tantalizing feathery touch that ignited more flames. And then his hand slipped between her legs. When he kissed her inner thighs, she spread her legs for him.

Slowly, thoroughly, he trailed kisses down her legs to her ankles and then turned her over to explore the backs of her legs, kissing her behind her knees, moving higher until he reached her nape. "Every inch of you is sexy and beautiful," he whispered.

Wanting him beyond measure, she rolled over to push him onto his back and then she returned his kisses, working her way down his chest, letting her tongue circle his flat nipples. Excited by his response as he wound his hands in her hair and groaned, she kissed his muscled, washboard belly. When he started to sit up, she pushed him down. She rubbed her pouty nipples against him and then ran her tongue around his shaft, letting her warm breath tantalize while her hands stroked his thighs. When she moved between his legs, he reached for her again, but she pushed his chest.

"You have to let me kiss you the way you kissed me," she whispered, shoving him down and continuing her rain of kisses until she rolled him over and worked her way along his back. When she kissed his inner thighs and played with his hard bottom, he twisted onto his back. She took his shaft into her mouth to stroke him with her tongue, slipping her hand between his legs to caress him.

"Olivia," he whispered, grinding out her name in a voice that was gravelly and thick. He was beaded with perspiration, aroused with his shaft rock hard and ready. He stood and held her in front of him while he stepped before a full-length mirror.

"Look how beautiful you are," he whispered, playing with her breasts, his hands dark against her pale skin. He kissed her nape and rubbed his shaft against her bottom and slid it between her legs to rub her.

She moaned with desire, whirling around to hold him. "I want you!" she cried, pulling his head down to kiss him passionately.

She hadn't thought it possible to want anyone to the degree she wanted Matt. She wanted to feel him inside her, to wrap her legs around him and love him through the night. Desire enveloped her, taking her breath and making her nerves raw. How could she want anyone this badly? Her hands swept over him in a feverish need.

"You're gorgeous," he whispered in her ear. "Look at us, Olivia."

Twisting around, she opened her eyes to meet his burning gaze in the mirror. The hunger in his expression took her breath and left no doubts that he wanted her. As he turned her to face him again, his blue eyes devoured her.

"I didn't know I could ever want a woman this badly," he said, and she didn't tell him she felt the same way about him. Words were lost as he swept her into his embrace, leaned over her and kissed her with such hunger she wondered exactly what he did feel for her.

How could he kiss her so wildly and not be falling in love?

She knew that he could do exactly that and still guard his heart. His hands and mouth and hot shaft drove everything from her mind except desire.

His kisses set off fireworks low inside her and sent flashes of light bursting behind her closed eyelids while every nerve tingled. She thrust her hips against his and closed her hand around his manhood, hoping to drive him beyond control.

He picked her up and carried her to bed, lowering her gently and then moving over her.

Spreading her legs for him, she opened her eyes to feast on the sight of him while her heart thudded. She ran her hands along his rock-hard thighs and then took his shaft in one hand as she sat up to run her tongue in slow circles around the velvet tip.

His hands wound in her hair again, shaking away the last of the pins and he groaned, letting her kiss and fondle him for a moment. With a groan he pushed her down.

Watching her, he moved between her thighs and then lifted her legs over his shoulders. His dark shaft throbbed with need. She looked up to meet his fiery gaze and then he lowered his head and his tongue stroked her most intimate places while his hands slipped over her bottom and between her legs.

Closing her eyes, she cried out with passion and arched her hips, thrashing wildly as need built to a raging inferno.

"Matt, love me! I want you to make love with me now. I can't wait longer," she cried out.

He leaned down and flicked his tongue around the curve of her ear. "Yes, you can wait," he whispered and let the tip of his tongue toy with her ear. "I want you really wild with no control at all, begging for love."

She wriggled away and sat up between his legs. "Two can do that," she whispered fiercely. She took his shaft in her mouth again, sliding it in and out and stroking him with her tongue.

He gasped and shoved her down, lowering himself. "Now," he whispered and she held him as the thick tip of his hard rod touched her.

She cried out and arched her hips, trying to pull him closer and wrapping her long legs tightly around him. "Love me, Matt!" she cried. "I want you! You don't know—"

He entered her slowly, filling her, hot and hard and driving her to wild abandon. Her head thrashed and her hips undulated in a rhythm to match his in an ageless dance of passion.

She was one with him, joined in body and now in marriage, falling more and more in love by the moment and devastated by his lovemaking.

Need burned her to cinders. "Matt, love me!" she gasped as he continued his slow torment, drawing his shaft out and then sliding into her in a scalding loving that heightened desire with each stroke.

Tension wound in her like a spring coiled tighter and tighter until she felt as if she would burst with the longing that drummed through her veins.

Sweat poured off him while she cried out and thrashed and nipped his shoulder. She clung to him, her hands sliding down his back, squeezing his hard buttocks. In abandon, she rocked with him.

Knowing that she was in love with this strong, sexy man who was taking her to paradise, she wanted to declare her love, but she bit back the words. She wasn't going to let him know that she had fallen in love with him when she was certain it would not be mutual and might not ever be returned. She didn't want his pity or sympathy.

Yet how difficult it was now, in the throes of the most passionate moment of her life, to avoid crying out her feelings and being totally open and honest with him.

His control vanished and he pumped into her, filling her hot and thick as they rocked together and spun to a blinding climax.

"Matt!" she cried, unaware of anything except his manhood and the sensations exploding from his loving.

"Olivia!" he gasped and covered her mouth, devouring her with another kiss that was a storm of passion.

All she knew was Matt, his body, his arms holding her, his thick rod inside her, filling her and joining them. She held him tightly as they finally slowed and then were still.

She caressed his damp back, sliding her hands down over the curve of his buttocks, down over the backs of his thighs, feeling the short dark hairs curl against her palms.

"You demolished me," she finally whispered.

He turned his head and she looked into his eyes. When she did, he leaned forward to kiss her. In seconds he pulled away. "You're fantastic,"

"Thank you," she answered quietly. "I'll say the same for you. We're a mutual admiration couple."

"One half of this couple is boneless and unable to move," he said, placing his head down on her bare shoulder and turning her on her side to face him. Their legs were tangled together and she toyed with locks of his hair with her free hand.

"It is great sex between us," she observed.

"You think so?" he asked solemnly.

"Yes," she answered in surprise. "You don't think so?"

"I don't know," he answered carefully. "In a few minutes we'll try again and see."

She hit his shoulder lightly. "You were teasing!" she exclaimed. "And I fell for it."

He chuckled softly. "We will try again, but not until I can move and lift my head."

"Lift your what?"

He laughed in a deep, throaty chuckle that conveyed his satisfaction. "Wildcat. You're trying to arouse me again."

"No, I'm not," she protested lightly. "When I try to arouse you again, you'll know it and it won't be just 'try'."

He nuzzled her neck and pulled her more closely against him. "This is good, Olivia. Better than I dreamed possible and I had high expectations."

"'High expectations' translates into you thought I was a bawdy wench," she remarked dryly, amused.

"Could be," he admitted, trailing kisses along her ear and throat. "We're not getting out of bed the rest of the week."

"That's what you think. Hunger will soon set in. I'm eating for two, you know. Now, I want to check out the beach. The water looks like the most inviting thing around here right now."

He hugged her. "I'm beginning to think you had a very good idea when you proposed to me. I should have thought of this."

Her heart leaped even though she knew he wasn't thinking about falling in love.

"Good! I don't have to have a guilty conscience about finagling you into marriage."

"I don't know. I like you to have a guilty conscience because then you'll do more to please me."

"Is that so? I better start learning what pleases you. Let's see—how's this?" she asked, kissing his neck lightly.

He groaned and pulled her close against him. "You give me a moment to catch my breath. I don't have a bone in my body that will function now. I can't stand. I can't even move." He smiled at her and raked her damp hair away from her face. "This is good, Olivia. It's a hell of a lot better than what I had planned for us."

"Good. I quite agree, but remember that when times get tough."

"So what's going to make times get tough?" he asked, arching his eyebrows. The humor had gone from his tone of voice.

"I don't know now, but you know there will be moments we won't agree. There have been a few already and we barely know each other."

"This is a fine arrangement for both of us. You'll get your law degree, I get to be a father and we'll give our baby a family. You couldn't ask for more."

She kept her mouth closed, but she knew she wanted a whole

lot more. She wanted his heart. She wanted him to fall in love because she was falling in love. She ran her hand along his muscled shoulder and the strong column of his neck, feeling the damp sweat still at his hairline. She couldn't get enough of touching him, kissing him and she wanted so much more from him than merely a fine, workable arrangement. Maybe with time, she thought, running her finger along his jaw and then so lightly across his lips. He bit her fingers gently and then kissed her forehead.

"Later, you can practice law in Rincon or even in Fort Worth which isn't a bad commute," he said.

"I'm not worrying about that now," she said. "I have to get through years of school before that time comes."

"If there are more babies, you may change your mind completely." She smiled at him, and they gazed at each other in satisfaction. To her surprise, he rolled away, stood and picked her up.

"I thought you were weak-kneed and all that," she exclaimed.

"I'm getting my strength back," he said. "Touching and looking at you is doing all sorts of things to revive me."

"Where are we going?" she asked, alarmed as he strode outside.

"This is a very private beach, remember? The only people here are on the other side of the island, so don't worry. Unless there's a low-flying plane, which there isn't, we have this strictly to ourselves."

He carried her into the water and finally it was deep enough that he let her legs down and slowly let her slide down the length of him to stand facing him. She felt his arousal, hot and hard against her in spite of the cold water.

"You're oversexed," she accused, teasing him.

"Only because of you," he rejoined and pulled her to him to kiss her. His hands slipped over her, tantalizing strokes that rekindled her desire and she caressed his smooth, wet body, finally slipping away from him.

"Come here," she said, laughing up at him and catching his hand.

He splashed back to the beach with her where she turned to wrap her arms around him and kiss him hungrily.

As if they hadn't made love, he swept her into his arms again and walked to a chaise. He sat and put her astride him. His hands cupped her breasts and his thumbs circled her nipples as his thick rod slid into her and filled her. She closed her eyes and gasped with pleasure, moving her hips.

Need built, driving her to move faster, tension coiling with each stroke of his manhood. She felt his fingers between her legs, rubbing her and creating more fires.

"Matt!" she cried out, moving wildly, pumping him until release burst in her with her climax. His hands held her hips as he still thrust and then he clutched her more tightly.

"Olivia! I want you!" he exclaimed deeply. He thrust rapidly, shuddering and she knew he had reached his climax.

She fell across him, gasping for breath. His breathing was as ragged as hers and she could hear her pounding pulse. Sunshine was hot on her back and he was hot beneath her.

"We need to get into the water to cool down again."

His arm circled her waist and he held her tightly against him. "Not quite yet. I want to hold you."

She smiled and raised her head to look down at him. He was bathed in sweat and his hair was a tangle of black locks across his forehead. Satisfaction filled his blue eyes and made her heart drum.

"I married a most handsome, sexy man," she said lightly, tracing her finger along his jaw.

He rolled her beside him, turning to face her. "And you're gorgeous and I don't want you to even open those bags you brought. I want you naked all week."

She laughed. "I think not! I carefully bought two new swimsuits—"

"I'll get them off you faster than you can get them on," he said, brushing hair away from her face. The ends were damp, but she hadn't done any swimming so the rest was dry.

"I've bought new clothes for this week."

"Show them to me back in Texas next week," he said.

"I'm not sitting around and eating in the nude."

"Shall we take bets?" he asked wickedly and she had to laugh.

"I'm perfectly willing to stay naked all week," he offered.

"I'll bet you are. Now that's not a bad thought but if you do, it'll mean we'll never get far from the bed or this chaise."

"I'll make that sacrifice," he teased. "It's good between us, Olivia."

She nodded. "It may just get better and better. Had you ever thought of that?"

He studied her and ran his finger down her cheek. "Maybe I can stagger into the water now if you keep me from drowning if I slide under."

"I'll keep you from drowning," she remarked and stood, walking toward the water and turning to see him sitting on the chaise watching her.

"You're not coming?"

"I was enjoying the view."

"Matt! Stop ogling me and come swim."

"I'd rather ogle," he said, standing and her gaze raked over him before she turned to go into the water. Her back tingled and her cheeks heated because she knew he was watching her closely. As soon as she was in waist deep water, she sank down to cool and turn to watch him stride casually into the water.

His body was muscled, male perfection, well-sculpted, tan. Just the sight of him made her pulse pound and rekindled her desire. "Come on in," she said.

Matt strolled leisurely out to her. He was exhausted and satisfied, but watching her just now, he knew that wasn't a condition that would last. Not with Olivia going around nude. He marveled at his good fortune. She was a fantastic lover with a body beyond belief. But he knew it was more than her body. She had a sexual air about her that was seduction just being around her.

The beach had a gradual slope and Olivia had walked out to a point where only her head and shoulders were above water. He joined her, reaching out to slip his arm around her narrow waist.

"I thought all this water would cool you down," she said, slanting him a saucy look.

"It should, but your naked body is a lot stronger influence and it heats me up. Touching you excites me," he said softly. "Looking at you excites me," he added. He gazed at her, infinitely thankful he hadn't gotten his way and settled for living under the same roof and nothing more.

And then he wondered if he was falling in love? Had she gotten past his barriers and reached his heart?

The idea startled him and he stared at her, wondering what he truly did feel for her and what it could develop into. Was he already in love with his new wife? Even when he had thought he was guarding his heart so well.

"Give me a few minutes," she said. "I recognize that look in your eye."

"You bring it on with your sexy walk and your bare bottom and long legs. Want to see?" he asked, stepping closer and rubbing against her, amazed himself at how easily she turned him on.

"I know there's something wrong with you," she remarked. "Duck yourself under the water and cool down." She turned to swim away from him and he followed, catching her and pulling her into his arms to kiss her while he treaded water and kept them both afloat.

"Don't you ever get enough?"

"I don't know," he answered. "This making love to you is all new to me, so we'll just have to see," he said before ducking his head to kiss her again.

To his surprise, he discovered that he couldn't get enough of her. They made love leisurely, and then quickly with a hungry passion that he wouldn't have thought possible when they had already loved so much.

That night, long after she had fallen asleep in his arms, he stirred and looked down at her, combing long locks of her hair away from her face while satisfaction filled him. She was sexy, beautiful and intelligent. She was going to give him babies and a marriage and solid family life. Gratitude filled him and he wondered how long it would take before he did fall in love with her. Or was he already there? Was he in love with his new wife?

They had barely eaten dinner and he was ravenous, but as he rolled over to kiss her awake, her warm, soft body aroused him and soon he was making love to her again and he forgot all about his stomach and food.

The next morning Olivia woke and shifted. She looked around, momentarily disoriented and then a strong, brown arm tightened around her waist and memories tumbled back. She looked at her sleeping husband who held her tightly. They had made love off and on since arriving and now her stomach was growling with hunger.

She slipped out of his embrace and went inside, switching on a small lamp and looking around at an inviting large bedroom with a king-size bed, bamboo furniture and a polished plank floor. She retrieved her bag, showered and pulled on a sheer black negligee she had bought and then went to the kitchen. She discovered it was fully stocked with food and dishes that had been cooked and were ready to heat. A fruit platter was in the refrigerator and she removed it, taking off the wrap that protected it and eating a thick chunk of delicious pineapple.

"There you are," Matt said and she turned to see him standing in the doorway.

He had showered and slicked back his wet hair and tied a white towel around his middle. Her pulse began to drum, but she picked up a strawberry and waved it at him.

"We are going to eat before I faint."

His mouth curved in a crooked smile as his gaze drifted down over her and she wished she had simply pulled on cutoffs and a T-shirt instead of the sheer, sexy negligee.

"Matt, we're going to eat. Did you hear me?"

"Sure. We'll eat, but you didn't dress like that and expect me to not notice, did you?" he said, strolling to her and her heart began a drumroll.

"You stay right here," she said, placing a hand against his

chest as she passed him and hurried from the room. She dashed to the bedroom, gathered clothes and changed.

Shortly she returned to the kitchen to find him getting out skewers with chunks of steak, mushrooms, onions and small tomatoes.

He placed them on plates and he already had glasses of water poured. "I heated these in the microwave. They've already been cooked and they should still be tasty."

"They'll be a feast," she said, trying to resist falling on it and devouring it as hunger tore at her. "I'm starved."

He studied her. "I liked the black thing better."

"I'll bet you did," she said, smiling at him and wondering how long the towel would stay tied around his middle, knowing if it lasted through breakfast, then she would remove it.

They were halfway through breakfast when she looked up to meet his smoldering blue gaze. She realized he was no longer eating, but looking at her with as much desire as if they had never made love. She lost all appetite and lowered her fork as he pushed away his chair and came around the table to take her into his arms.

"I feel like it's been a day instead of an hour since we made love," he said, kissing her throat.

She turned her head to kiss him, winding her arms around his neck and all thoughts of breakfast were forgotten.

Three days later Olivia was stretched beside him on a chaise after making love. "It may be difficult to return to reality."

"If you'd like to stay longer, we can, but you'll love the Argentine ranch. It's spectacular. We can stay here or on the ranch as long as we want.

"Don't you have to get back?"

"I told you that we're buying the ranch in Argentina. I stay there or on the California ranch a good part of the year."

She sat up to look at him. "What about the Texas ranch?"

He gave her a crooked smile and toyed with locks of her hair. He was stretched out with a towel across his middle and she wore a two-piece red swimsuit. "We have a foreman, but usually I go back after a few months to keep Dad happy. He wants me to run the ranch and as long as he's alive, I don't stay away more than a couple of months at a time."

Surprised, she studied him. "What do you mean by, 'As long as he's alive'?"

"After Dad's gone, I'll probably turn the Texas ranch over to Sandy full-time and move to Argentina. I love that ranch— it's beautiful country. I'll go home for board meetings for Ransome Energy, but I don't have to live there."

"You didn't tell me this," she said stiffly.

His eyes narrowed. "I think I mentioned the ranches. Besides, Dad will be around, probably until our baby is grown, so it really doesn't matter."

"It matters a lot," she said. "And you never know what tomorrow will bring. You told me about buying a ranch in Argentina, but you didn't tell me that that's where you prefer to live."

His hand stilled. "This is going to be a problem?"

"Indeed, it is," she said, her temper rising. "You should have told me."

"This won't happen for years. Look, Dad's alive. It would hurt him if I didn't run the Texas ranch, so as long as he's living, I'm not going to stay away any great length of time. He should be around many more years. You're conjuring up something that doesn't exist at the present."

"Your father has had one heart attack and you can't say what will happen to any of us on any given day. A vacation now and then would be fabulous. To live there—no way."

"It's as good a life as in Texas," he said in a cold, quiet tone that chilled her even more.

She shook her head. "No, it isn't. I want a regular life and regular school in the U.S."

"Okay, Olivia. We can settle it when the time comes."

"Somehow that's not much reassurance," she said, trying to curb her anger.

"I'm redoing an eight-bedroom ranch house in Argentina right now. Even with Dad alive and at the ranch, I intend to stay in the new ranch house, once it's finished, at least two months out of the year. I want my child to go with me. Dad knows I do this every year and that's all right. I do a couple of months on that ranch and it brings in a hell of an income so Dad's fine with it."

"That's disruptive and I can't leave school and later I can't leave a job."

"Look, we're married. You don't even have to go to school any longer and you sure as hell don't have to practice law or work for someone else."

She stood up. "You should have told me. I'm not letting you take my baby off to Argentina for months and I'm not giving up law school because you prefer that ranch to the three others that you own."

"So what the hell are you going to do?"

She stared at him with her anger boiling and hurt simmering that he hadn't told her about his preference in ranches or his plans for the future. "I'll have to figure that one out, Matt, but I'm ready to get out of here." She swept past him and into the house, going straight to get her bags, feeling she should pack and get someone to fly her away from the island before she really lost it and said things to Matt she would regret. How could he possibly think she would take her child to go live in South America, isolated on a ranch for a large part of the year? She steamed with anger because he hadn't leveled with her about his plans.

Tossing her clothes into the bag, she turned to gather more and saw Matt standing in the doorway watching her. He had tied the towel around his middle.

"Can you get a plane for me?" she asked stiffly, gathering more of her things. "I don't want to stay here any longer."

Anger flashed in his eyes and a muscle worked in his jaw. "I'll fly you back myself." He turned away and in minutes she saw him on the patio talking on his cell phone.

She wasn't giving up getting her education. She had seen the anger in his expression and she didn't think he was going to change one aspect of his life either and she realized they should have spent more time talking about their lives. She tossed her shirts and shorts into her bag. She had spent time talking to him. He knew about her law school plans and her desire to practice law. She just hadn't known anything about his goals for his future.

Anger made her shake. She didn't think he had been up-front and straight with her. She didn't know what she would do when they reached Texas. Was she walking out of this marriage already?

She knew she wouldn't do that if he went to Argentina to live forever and she never saw him again. Marriage still gave her baby a future and it gave her a chance for law school that she might not ever have worked out otherwise. No, she would stay, but she could see all hopes for love or a happy marriage smashing into a million pieces that couldn't be put together again.

Matt had acquiesced to her wishes to get the baby into the Ransome family, but he wouldn't consent to her wishes on this. She had no illusions about that. He wouldn't care what she did at this point.

She dressed in emerald slacks and a matching emerald linen top and caught her hair behind her head in a ponytail, tying it with a bright emerald scarf.

"The plane will be ready in an hour, Olivia," Matt said from the doorway.

She nodded. "Sorry, but I know what I want," she said quietly.

"You always have," he replied and they stared at each other and she could feel the clash of wills that was as strong as that first night they had met. She picked up her bag and swept past him.

"I'm out of the bedroom if you want it to yourself," she said.

She went to the front to set down her bag. Hurting, she paced the room, looking around her and suspecting she would never be back here again.

A little over an hour later, she was buckled into a seat in the plane and Matt was up front at the controls. She wondered how good a pilot he was, but then guessed that he was probably quite good. He had hardly spoken on the way to the airport and she could feel the waves of anger that buffeted her.

Tears threatened, but no matter how she looked at it, she

didn't see changing her mind about her future and tossing aside
her education. If she didn't get one and Matt sent her packing
one day, without an education, she would be back at jobs like
she'd had in the past.

And she knew without question she wasn't letting him take
her baby out of the country for months at a time, no matter how
productive the ranch was or how beautiful. Not during a school
year when a child would have to be tutored.

When they landed, she was no closer to solving the problems
facing them and she could see he wasn't either or he wouldn't
look as if he were trying to bank his fury.

At the ranch house he took the bags and she went on to her
room so she could be alone.

Matt set his bag in his room and then carried hers to knock
on her door. When she called to come in, he stepped inside and
faced her. The tension was thick between them. His anger was
palpable and she raised her chin, ready for a fight with him. She
hurt and could feel something precious and vital slipping out
of her life.

"Here's your bag. Where do we go from here, Olivia?"

"I don't know. I'll have to give it thought. I want to stay married."

"I'm sure you do. Well, we have a deal, and I'll stick by it,"
he said gruffly and then left abruptly.

Matt strode down the hall and outside, beginning to jog to
work off his frustration. He wondered if she really would stay.
He expected her to walk out. It hadn't ever occurred to him to
talk to her about the ranch in Argentina. His dad was alive and
well and Argentina on a permanent basis was far in the future.
Too far to give much thought to now. She could get her degree
and practice law. He hadn't foreseen that his plans to live in Argentina years from now would be a problem. To stay a couple
of months a year hadn't seemed unreasonable either.

She could go on with her life and he with his, but he wanted
to take the baby with him a lot of the time and she obviously
was going to try to block that every way she could.

Was he wrong? He didn't think he was being unreasonable and a lot of women would have loved it if they had the opportunities that he was providing for Olivia.

"Dammit!" he snapped and kicked a rock as he jogged. Let her go and to hell with her, he told himself, but even as he did, he thought about the past days since the wedding and how great life had been with her. He hurt badly and he had to admit that he wanted her in his life.

He ran for over two hours and finally returned to the house. He had no idea where she was, but he wasn't going to pursue her when she wouldn't want him to.

For the next two days he didn't see any sign of her until he began to wonder if she had packed and moved out without telling him, but at night he could hear her moving around in her room. He had no idea where she ate or what she was doing.

Then Saturday morning, a week after their wedding, he was walking down the hall when her door swung open. She was white and her eyes were round. She grasped the doorjamb and clung to it.

"Olivia! What's wrong?" he asked, forgetting their argument.

"I'm going to the emergency room," she answered weakly and then her knees buckled.

Twelve

His heart thudded as Matt swept her up in his arms. He carried her downstairs to his car where he placed her on the backseat. With rising panic, he dashed around to climb behind the wheel and race down the drive. Terror made him cold as he picked up his cell phone and punched numbers with one hand while he steered the car with the other.

"Who's your doctor, Olivia?"

"Dr. Porter. I've called him and he's meeting me at Rincon General."

Matt called 911 and talked to the dispatcher, giving directions to the ranch.

"We're headed to town. Send an ambulance to meet us. I'll see it coming. I'm driving a black four-door." He replaced the receiver and gripped the wheel glancing in the rearview mirror.

"How're you doing?" he asked her. "What's wrong?"

"I don't know. I have cramps and I'm faint and woozy," she answered. His heart thudded. He was frightened for the baby, frightened for Olivia. He prayed they would both be all right.

He sped down the ranch road and spun out on the highway, heading into town and listening for an ambulance. He saw it coming long before he heard it and he slowed, pulling off the road and getting out to flag it down. As it approached he stepped into the road and waved his arms.

Slowing, the ambulance pulled off and in minutes they were loading Olivia into the back. Matt held her hand. "Hang on, dar-lin'," he said, giving her hand a squeeze. "I'll follow and I'll be there with you."

The ambulance made a slow, careful U-turn and headed back the way it had come at a much slower speed.

With a pounding heart, Matt hunched over the wheel and followed, wanting to step on the gas and get her where she would have help.

At the emergency entrance, he watched helplessly while they wheeled her inside and then directed him to a waiting room. Rubbing his neck, praying she and the baby were all right, he paced the room. Fear gripped him. It was over an hour before a nurse called his name and he hurried across the room.

"Dr. Porter can talk to you and you can go see your wife. It's the third room on the right through those double doors."

"Thanks," he called over his shoulder, already jogging the direction she had pointed. Matt found the tall, thin, brown-haired doctor coming out of a room and he introduced himself.

"She's fine," Dr. Porter said. "Or she will be."

"She didn't look or feel fine," Matt snapped, wondering if she had received the care she should have.

The physician smiled. "She hasn't been eating right. It's a matter of getting the right fluids back in her. We'll keep her tonight and release her in the morning and if she'll take care of herself—or you take care of her—she'll be back to normal in no time."

As relief poured through him, Matt felt weak in the knees. "Thanks," he said. "Can I see her?"

"Yes, but she's dozed off. She's malnourished and what-ever's been bothering her, I told her she needs to stop worrying about it until after this baby arrives," he said and Matt realized the talk was directed at him.

"I understand. Thanks," Matt repeated. He moved past the doctor and went inside, walking quietly. Olivia had an IV dripping a solution that went into her arm and she lay still with her eyes closed. Matt wanted to kick himself.

He felt as if he had caused this as much as if he had withheld food and water from her. He knew that wasn't the case, she had done this to herself, but he felt responsible. And he realized she was important to him. She had given him a dreadful scare, both for her and the baby, but he had been terrified for her and he realized she was far more important to him than he had admitted to himself.

And she was more important than living on their Argentina ranch or any other damn thing like that in his life. He'd stuck it out on the Texas ranch the majority of the time for his dad. He could do that for Olivia and the baby. They were the most important people in his life now.

That thought startled him, but he realized it was true. He moved a chair beside the bed and sat down, taking her hand in his. "I love you," he said quietly, knowing she couldn't hear him, but he wanted to say it. He raised her hand to his lips and brushed a feathery kiss across her knuckles. "Get well, darlin'," he whispered.

She turned her head and opened her eyes to look at him. "Matt?"

"I'm here," he said. "Go back to sleep."

She stared at him and he leaned over the bed to kiss her lightly on the mouth. He sat down again, still holding her hand. "Go to sleep. You and the baby are going to be fine."

She nodded and closed her eyes.

Matt called the ranch and settled in the vinyl chair, watching her breathe and thinking she looked weak and vulnerable. He wanted to pull her into his arms and hold her, but he knew that wouldn't help her.

That night he slept in the chair by her bed and when he stirred the next morning, Olivia was gazing at him with curiosity.

"Hi," he said, leaning forward to kiss on her forehead. He took her hand in his.

"Hi," she answered. "You were here all night?"

"Yep. How're you feeling?"

"Better. I guess they've been giving me something."

"Your doc said you haven't been eating right."

"I suppose not."

"We'll remedy that," he said quietly. "I'll start cooking for you. But then, maybe my cooking will be an improvement and maybe it won't be," he said, and she smiled.

"I want to get out of here."

"They said you could go this morning."

The door opened and a nurse appeared and Matt stood. "I'll come back, Olivia. I'll wait in the hall." He stepped outside, going to get a cup of coffee.

The morning seemed long and tedious but by half past ten, Olivia was dismissed. They brought her down to his car in a wheelchair. She moved to the car to buckle herself into the passenger seat.

"I'm better," she said as soon as he pulled away from the hospital entrance. "Thanks for going with me."

He reached over to take her hand. "You're not going to skip any meals after this."

"No, I won't."

"Do you want something to eat now?"

"Goodness no. They removed the IV and then brought me breakfast. I couldn't eat another bite."

He glanced at her and saw to his relief, that her color was good and she looked like herself except thinner and he wondered if she had eaten at all since returning from Ariel.

He turned in the park and drove beneath a tall live oak that provided cool shade beneath it's arching branches. He cut the motor and turned to Olivia who looked at him with curiosity. "What are you doing?"

He lowered the windows to let in a morning breeze and turned in the seat to take her hand. "You gave me a hell of a scare."

"I've been eating, but I guess not enough. I thought I was taking care of myself."

He kissed her knuckles and ran them along his cheek.

Olivia could feel the rough stubble on his jaw. He hadn't shaved and his clothes were rumpled, his hair tangled. She thought she had heard him tell her that he loved her, but she wondered if she had imagined it or it had been medication they had given her that caused a delusion. Worry clouded Matt's blue eyes and she wondered what was on his mind. She wished she knew whether he had really declared his love or not.

As if reading her mind, he slipped his arm around her waist. "I love you."

She closed her eyes. How she had dreamed of him saying that! Now it didn't matter because they couldn't work out a future together. Tears threatened and she had received a lecture from her doctor about her attitude.

"Olivia," Matt said in a husky voice, "will you marry me?"

Surprised, she opened her eyes wide and stared at him. "We're married, remember?"

He gave her a faint smile. "I remember, but you proposed and I wasn't in love."

Her heart started drumming as she stared at him.

"This time, I'm proposing to the woman I love."

"What about living in Argentina on your family ranch instead of the Texas one?"

"I've always given that up for Dad. I can give it up for you and our baby. It won't mean much to me without you there. Will you marry me?"

Stunned and overwhelmed, she stared at him while tears spilled down her cheeks. He wiped them away. "Don't cry, darlin'. I didn't intend to make you cry."

She smiled and put her arms around his neck. "They're tears of joy, Matt. Of course, I'll marry you, but we don't need to do that. Your declaration of love is the world to me! I don't want to plan another wedding."

"Whatever you want. If you do, okay. If you don't, okay. I just want you to know that I love you and I want you to be my wife."

She hugged him again, feeling as if weights had been lifted from her heart. "Matt, you've just made me the happiest woman in the world!" she cried, tears spilling down her cheeks.

"You don't act happy, darlin'. You're crying—"

"I told you, they're tears of joy, believe me. I love you, too, Matt Ransome. I'm going to make you the happiest man on earth."

He chuckled. "Maybe in bed. Sometimes, though, I suspect you're going to worry the socks off me the way you've done in the short time I've known you. Since meeting you, darlin', my peaceful life has gone out the window."

She smiled at him. "I'm worth it," she said, and he laughed.

"Yes, you are," he said and then bent his head to kiss her.

Overjoyed, Olivia clung to him while her heart thudded with so much joy she felt as if she would burst. "Let's go back for another honeymoon that won't be cut short," she whispered.

"Sounds like a deal to me," he said and smiled, leaning down to kiss her again.

Epilogue

The following January as wind howled and snow swirled, blanketing Rincon, inside a hospital delivery room, a baby's cry filled the air. "Here's your boy," Dr. Porter said, placing a small baby on Olivia's stomach.

Matt leaned over the baby. "He's perfect!"

Olivia smiled. "I think so, too."

The nurse picked up the baby to clean him up.

"Jefferson Matthew Ransome," Olivia said.

Matt grinned broadly and bent to kiss his wife. "You have a perfect baby," he said softly.

"We have a perfect baby," she reminded him, and he gazed at her with love in his eyes.

He straightened up. "I've got to tell the family. They're all coming to see little Jeff Ransome."

"You'd think no one ever had a baby before," Olivia said, looking at banks of flowers that had already arrived from Matt's father and Kathcrine and Nick. "Look at all these flowers, and that was before Jeff was born."

"Dad's outside and can't wait to get in here to see you."

"Phooey, Matt. He doesn't want to see me. He wants to see Jeff."

"He'll be happy with you for giving him Jeff."

Olivia smiled at her tall, handsome husband and thought how good life had become for her. Now she had a baby son that she and Matt could love. Matt took Olivia's hand.

"I'm leaving for a few minutes, but I'll be back soon," he said.

She nodded and watched him stride out of the room and joy filled her over her baby and over Matt being in her life. Thirty minutes later he returned and crossed the room to her bed. "Are they finished working on you?"

"Yes, they are."

"Then Dad wants to see you. Sandy and some of the guys are here, and Katherine's flying in if the blizzard doesn't ground planes. Nick will arrive tonight."

"That's great. I'm glad Jeff has arrived in a family that will love him."

"We're going to love him so much, it'll make your head spin."

"You're not going to spoil him to pieces," Olivia said, and Matt grinned. His blue eyes twinkled as he pulled a box from his pocket and placed it in Olivia's hand.

"This is for you, darlin'," he said, and she opened a black velvet box. She gasped with surprise and delight when she lifted out a diamond and emerald bracelet.

"It's beautiful, Matt!" she exclaimed. "Just gorgeous."

He leaned down to take her in his arms and she hugged him. "Not half as beautiful as my wife," he said quietly. "I love you, Olivia. You're my world and my life now."

His words thrilled her, and Olivia clung to his broad shoulders as she turned her face up for his kiss. Her love for him made her heart pound with joy and she held him tightly, eager to be home in his arms again, knowing when she married him, she had made the best choice of her life.

* * * * *

In October 2006, look for
REVENGE OF THE SECOND SON,
Nick Ransome's provocative story.

Set in darkness beyond the ordinary world.
Passionate tales of life and death.
With characters' lives ruled by laws the everyday world can't
begin to imagine.

Introducing NOCTURNE, *a spine-tingling*
new line from Silhouette Books.

The thrills and chills begin with
UNFORGIVEN by Lindsay McKenna

Plucked from the depths of hell, former military sharpshooter
Reno Manchahi was hired by the government to kill a thief, but
he had a mission of his own. Descended from a family of shape-
shifters, Reno vowed to get the revenge he'd thirsted for all
these years. But his mission went awry when his target turned
out to be a powerful seductress, Magdalena Calen Hernandez,
who risked everything to battle a potent evil. Suddenly, Reno had
to transform himself into a true hero and fight the enemy that
threatened them all. He had to become a Warrior for the Light....

Turn the page for a sneak preview of
UNFORGIVEN by Lindsay McKenna.
On sale September 26, wherever books are sold.

One

One shot...one kill.

The sixteen-pound sledgehammer came down with such fierce power that the granite boulder shattered instantly. A spray of glittering mica exploded into the air and sparkled momentarily around the man who wielded the tool as if it were a weapon. Sweat ran in rivulets down Reno Manchahi's drawn, intense face. Naked from the waist up, the hot July sun beating down on his back, he hefted the sledgehammer skyward once more. Muscles in his thick forearms leaped and biceps bulged. Even his breath was focused on the boulder. In his mind's eye, he pictured Army General Robert Hampton's fleshy, arrogant fifty-year-old features on the rock's surface. Air exploded from between his lips as he brought the avenging hammer down. The boulder pulverized beneath his funneled hatred.

One shot...one kill...

Nostrils flaring, he inhaled the dank, humid heat and drew it deep into his massive lungs. Revenge allowed Reno to endure his imprisonment at a U.S. Navy brig near San Diego, California. Drops of sweat were flung in all directions as the crack of his sledgehammer claimed a third stone victim. Mouth taut, Reno moved to the next boulder.

The other prisoners in the stone yard gave him a wide berth. They always did. They instinctively felt his simmering hatred, the palpable revenge in his cinnamon-colored eyes, was more than skin-deep.

And they whispered he was different.

Reno enjoyed being a loner for good reason. He came from a medicine family of shape-shifters. But even this secret power had not protected him—or his family. His wife, Ilona, and his three-year-old daughter, Sarah, were dead. Murdered by Army General Hampton in their former home on USMC base in Camp Pendleton, California. Bitterness thrummed through Reno as he savagely pushed the toe of his scarred leather boot against several smaller pieces of gray granite that were in his way.

The sun beat down upon Manchahi's naked shoulders, grown dark red over time, shouting his half-Apache heritage. With his straight black hair grazing his thick shoulders, copper skin and broad face with high cheekbones, everyone knew he was Indian. When he'd first arrived at the brig, some of the prisoners taunted him and called him Geronimo. Something strange happened to Reno during his fight with the name-calling prisoners. Leaning down after he'd won the scuffle, he'd snarled into each of their bloodied faces that if they were going to call him anything, they would call him *gan,* which was the Apache word for *devil*.

His attackers had been shocked by the wounds on their faces, the deep claw marks. Reno recalled doubling his fist as they'd attacked him en masse. In that split second, he'd gone into an altered state of consciousness. In times of danger, he transformed into a jaguar. A deep, growling sound had emitted from his throat as he defended himself in the three-against-one fracas. It all happened so fast that he thought he had imagined it. He'd seen his hands morph into a forearm and paw, claws extended. The slashes left on the three men's faces after the fight told him he'd begun to shape-shift. A fist made bruises and swelling; not four perfect, deep claw marks. Stunned and anxious, he hid the knowledge of what else he was from these prisoners. Reno's only defense was to make all the prisoners so damned scared of him and remain a loner.

Alone. Yeah, he was alone, all right. The steel hammer swept downward with hellish ferocity. As the granite groaned in protest, Reno shut his eyes for just a moment. Sweat dripped off his nose and square chin.

Straightening, he wiped his furrowed, wet brow and looked into the pale blue sky. What got his attention was the startling cry of a red-tailed hawk as it flew over the brig yard. Squinting, he watched the bird. Reno could make out the rust-colored tail on the hawk. As a kid growing up on the Apache reservation in Arizona, Reno knew that all animals that appeared before him were messengers.

Brother, what message do you bring me? Reno knew one had to ask in order to receive. Allowing the sledgehammer to drop to his side, he concentrated on the hawk who wheeled in tightening circles above him.

Freedom! the hawk cried in return.

Reno shook his head, his black hair moving against his broad, thickset shoulders. *Freedom? No way, Brother. No way.* Figuring that he was making up the hawk's shrill message, Reno turned away. Back to his rocks. Back to picturing Hampton's smug face.

Freedom!

* * * * *

*Look for UNFORGIVEN by Lindsay McKenna,
the spine-tingling launch title from Silhouette Nocturne ™.
Available September 26, wherever books are sold.*

If you enjoyed what you just read,
then we've got an offer you can't resist!

Take 2 bestselling love stories FREE!

Plus get a FREE surprise gift!

COMING NEXT MONTH

#1753 FORBIDDEN MERGER—Emilie Rose
The Elliotts
When a business tycoon falls for the one woman he can't have, their secret affair threatens to stir up *more* than a few hot nights.

#1754 BLACKHAWK'S BETRAYAL—Barbara McCauley
Secrets!
Mixing business with pleasure was not on her agenda...but bedding the boss may be the key to discovering the truth about her family.

#1755 THE PART-TIME WIFE—Maureen Child
Secret Lives of Society Wives
A society wife learns her husband is leading a double life and gets whisked into his world of scandals and secrets.

**#1756 THE MORNING-AFTER PROPOSAL—
Sheri WhiteFeather**
The Trueno Brides
He vowed to protect her under one condition—she become his wife. Will she succumb to her desires and his zealous proposal?

#1757 REVENGE OF THE SECOND SON—Sara Orwig
The Wealthy Ransomes
This billionaire bets he can seduce his rival's stunning granddaughter, until the tables turn and *she* raises the stakes.

**#1758 THE BOSS'S CHRISTMAS SEDUCTION—
Yvonne Lindsay**
Sleeping with the boss she secretly loved was not the best career move. Now she had to tell him she was expecting his baby.